Hands
Over
Time

60 Hands on 30 Fateful Journeys

Mark M. Dean

Monday Creek Publishing LLC
mondaycreekpublishing.com

My hands will forever hold dear those people who said I could.

Contents

Introduction

An amazing thing, the human hand. Even to this day our most talented engineers and scientists attempt to replicate its form, function and intricacies for people who may have been born without a hand or lost one to accident or disease. For centuries, artists, from the most famous to the most basic, have selected the hand as an object to master. The talent to replicate the hand has created masterpieces, or a lack of talent has driven many to other forms of art. How many times have you, sitting there right now, using your hands, have sat for minutes trying to remember what caused a certain scar on your finger or palm? Do gypsies and fortunetellers really know what those lines and creases represent? Oh, and the many things you can do! Embellish stories, make rude gestures, sooth a crying baby, make a fabulous dinner for your family, welcome or bid farewell to a loved one.

Hands Over Time celebrates the use of our hands in 30 short stories by giving you a glimpse into the personal thoughts of 30 unique situations. Of all the connections our mental and physical attributes share, the one that fascinates me most is between the mind and hands. Yes, there are others, but this relationship is the most practical, the most direct, with the ability to physically connect our emotions to our actions.

Now it's time you will your fingers to touch the corner of the page, turn it, and get a glimpse into some unique thoughts.

Just One More

I've always been enthralled with books people have given me. From family members to church folk, to those I've met in passing. I don't know, perhaps I've always enjoyed seeing how other people interpret a book and how at the end you either agree with them or think "Did we even read the same thing?" On the other hand, if I receive a novel of *War and Peace* proportions, I see this as akin to torture. Short, sweet, bite-sized; that's what I enjoy.

Clutching this new book in my hands, I've got that feeling. The instinctive one, the one from the gut telling me I just might like the words and stories within.

First off, I just love the cover. Now tattered and worn but reminiscent of the days it bore the smooth glossy finish of a new edition. The lifestyle photo adorning the cover truly captivates, foreshadowing the depth of the author's desire to wrestle me to the ground, captured in time. The hope, the sadness, the joy, the pure delight in living, perhaps? All sandwiched between two beat-up coffee-stained covers.

I sure wish I had kept track of the times someone in the family has picked up this little gem to read it outright, or maybe a small portion at a time. Either way, if I had to guess, my family has read this book 322, maybe even 323 times. Hard to tell. What I do know is the stories within, the succinct and powerful vignettes, never cease to start a conversation around the dinner table.

I carefully plan my time regarding these pieces of paper, glue and ink. Never in a hurry. Well honestly, at first, I was in a hurry. Which is no surprise to anyone close to me. However, my fidgeting nature has quieted somewhat over the years and I want to have the option, the luxury if you will, to mull over the characters, the genre, and, of course, how each story may in some way apply to me.

Looking back at my early childhood, I recognize that I had absolutely no patience. None. Zero. Nada. Every Christmas morning, I would tear through my presents in a fraction of the time it took my parents to wrap them. And the candy? It stood no chance at all. None. Zero. Nada. Wrappers flying all over the place, my dog strategically looming close by, his tail thumping, signifying his readiness for the collateral damage of my hurried feast. No patience at all.

I distinctly remember the first time I read this beloved book. Couldn't read it fast enough. I wanted to devour the whole thing immediately. None of this one chapter at a time crap. And then it bit me. Literally bit me. Like a puppy who finally says "Enough! You're playing too rough!" and lays a deep gash in your finger with those razor-sharp puppy teeth.

Well, the teeth marks of this little book came in the form of a vicious papercut. A warning sign, no doubt, that I was going too damn fast. At the very tip of my right index finger. Just where I would swipe my cellphone screen or click the computer mouse. How'd it know my tender uncalloused fingertip was vulnerable in that very spot?

Expletives went flying. Soliciting a well-timed "What's going on in there?" which floated in from the kitchen as dishes clattered and clanked in the sink.

"This freakin' book just took a chunk out of my finger!" I retorted with a bit too much attitude.

"Read it slower, you'll enjoy it more."

"After I get a tourniquet for my finger, I'm gonna read just one more chapter tonight." I only partially committed to that, knowing my binging nature.

A smudged bloody fingerprint still marks the first time I dug in. I should have written down the date and time. Not to sound too corny, but that was the very moment my life changed. Honestly.

I believe for each one of us on this spinning rock we call Earth, while journeying through humanity, the Greater Eternal Being reaches into our lives, pinches the little metal thingy at the end of the light string with His all-knowing fingers and gently pulls down on our light cord. For a brief moment in time, so brief it can't be measured in our limited minds, a light flickers.

Now I imagine this light as being an old-time light bulb. The ones that *buzzzzzes* and pops and then comes to life. During your enlightening process, if you will, The All Knowing, All Powerful recognizes within you whether your soul has taken on this new torch. If so, I can vividly see those fingers letting go of the string, hand and arm gracefully falling to His side, while the corners of His lips curve upward as the glowing, buzzing and popping light becomes part of you for the rest of your living days.

But, and here's the critical part, if The Timeless Being realizes you have not accepted His gift, at that very moment in unmeasurable time, the pressure in His fingertips increases, and with a slight tug on the white cord, pulls down, and that particular light is gone, perhaps to return when the pupil is ready. The string gently sways in the air, free of any pressure and His hand leaves the cord. The candle of discovery is snuffed out, an opportunity lost.

No opportunity lost for me. None. Zero. Nada. This object now resting in my hands, weighing less than a pound, lit a full-fledged bonfire within me. It cracked the door and let the light flood in as to the minds and thoughts of others. It gently brushed back the dusty cobwebs keeping those possibilities from me. Each time I pick the book up now, I realize how much more is hiding beyond the grimy window. How much deeper the pool is. As my eyes scan across the words, my mind recites them aloud, a habit since childhood, and each and every time, they seem to take on new meaning. My mind's fingertips are gently rubbing away the grit and grime on the window, allowing me to see through a pinhole, then a peephole, and perhaps eventually one entire windowpane in a mansion made of glass.

As my fingernail gently scratches the tip of my nose, adjusting my reading glasses, this book lives before me. Asking me, no, prodding me, with the question…

"Do we really know what others are thinking?"

What *is* the personal internal conversation we all have with ourselves and never share with anyone? Even the ones we love and cherish the most?

Ahhh, but what about the brazen and bold who are born without a filter? The ones who share every thought born in their minds. I dare say, for the multitudes, myself included, we find our hands gently pushing them away, keeping their nonfiltered, truth-belching ramblings at a safe distance.

Sinking into my cherished cracked leather recliner, I engage my entire being and quickly find my smudged fingerprint from many years ago. For now, I will remain disciplined, reading one story at a time. I have learned to enjoy this experience.

Venturing with the author into the mental ramblings of the mind of another who has also been delicately placed upon this earth. I know when I finish my one self-rationed story, I, too, will relax and let my mind create the thoughts of another, not mentioned in the pages of this beloved book. Creating a movie-sized drama as my characters' thoughts engage their hands, pulling, pushing and carrying them through a journey.

Your hands are now gently holding a new book, a new experience. Your mind is eager to delve into the thoughts of another. This is just the first of 30 individual internal conversations being laid bare one thought at a time, one page at a time, one story at a time.

As I watch my hands rest upon the keyboard of my laptop; scarred, inexperienced fingers tap out the first of many chapters. I visualize your light illuminating and beginning to flicker from the words and pages of my first novel *Hands Over Time*.

Puzzle Queen

Lifelines? Can I ever really call them that anymore?

I remember my baby's tiny, tiny fingers the day she was born; clutching, grabbing, feeling, trying to find the captive walls of my womb. Our true alone time coming to an abrupt end as she gulped her first breath. Mother-daughter alone time. What precious moments.

For the most part I had cherished alone time with my Mom. Particularly as a teenager. Relaxing and chatting about boys. Other times, more hostile and combative, when I was finding myself. The pure heat of those emotional times I can now appreciate.

I so look forward to all those experiences my baby and I will share. True solitude, communicating and bonding.

Those tiny palms were so soft and creased just like mine. Little baby lifelines, love lines. My Lord, I miss her.

Get your shit together and focus. Adult-onset ADD? Yea, sign me up.

My hands are so warm when I start. I think it's the heat from the stress which I can feel in my cheeks, brow, and back as it radiates through my body. It's probably the mental energy it takes to stuff all my emotions deep into my body. Not to mention the energy it takes to screw on my game face. The deeper the better, like I'm putting a boot on the throat of my emotions, stomping my feelings into submission.

I can't stand my hands smelling like those damn latex gloves at the end of the day. I wonder if other folks notice it? I scrub and scrub but it radiates through my nostrils. Kinda like when one of my teammates comes back from a smoke break. Some smell like cigarette smoke, but some smell like nicotine is oozing from every pore. The wretched latex smell seeps from my hands and arms. Makes me want to vomit hours later when I catch a whiff.

Focus…#122 is goin' be tough. She may have been a Mom, a sister, a lover.

All these dudes around me said I'd get numb to this shit. When's that gonna happen?

When's that going to happen, Jesus?

Man, the cold in here makes my knuckles ache. I haven't even begun yet and they are starting to throb. How much of this is mental anyway? Hmmm, do I smell like rubber? Are my knuckles aching? Or am I in some nightmare?

Wish someone could turn the heat up just a little bit.

Ahhh, found her. The bag tag always flutters as it slips through my fingers. Twisting and turning like a leaf falling from a tree in the autumn, not sure which way it wants to go. Name up? Name down? Your decision Ms Tag.

My hand still shakes as I touch the zipper, instantly bonding our stories, our histories. My fingers know to yank first, pulling hard and away, thus committing my soul to hers. The gate to my personal hell silently swings open with the *szzzerrrpping* sound. My hell's gate doesn't creak and groan like in a horror movie. No, mine is too well oiled.

And there you are, my friend.

Damn, what a fucking mess, God Damn IEDs! Simple contraptions now. One call from a cellphone or push of a button and worlds are blown apart, extinguished, and changed forever. Not just next to the smoking hole either, all over the world. At that time, at that moment. Some just don't know it yet. Those innocent lives are dropping kids off at school, playing golf, organizing a Yellow Ribbon event welcoming their soldiers home.

The whole right side of your body is shredded Ma'am. You must have been riding shotgun when you got hit.

I notice the rubber gloves at the end of my arms brushing her hair back, through the caked blood and dirt. My gentle fingertip dabbing her

11

cheek where her mascara had run, during those last terrifying, then peaceful moments.

How beautiful you are, even in death. Death.

Thank goodness your face only has a few cuts. I can clean those up for you, no problem. Be happy to, as it'll make a huge difference when they first see you at home. "Be happy to?" Really? Did I just think that?

Glad Mom insisted I take piano; my tiny fingers can dance around this wreckage and make some semblance of life reappear. Presto! I wonder what she looked like when she laughed and cried with those who were most dear to her?

High cheekbones, jet black hair, definitely Hispanic, or perhaps Native American? I can't stand performing the inventory. Always so calculating. My hands taking on a tender life of their own. Always amazed at how a body part can do that. Legs walking, eyes blinking, all moving right along like they have a mind of their own.

Ok, I feel it, the right leg is mangled, but attached, I can work with that. There's the ankle, not too bad.

All right, Honey, bad news, I only count three little piggies. Yikes, my pointer almost caught that shard of glass, let's pick that out. *Ting...* it goes in the highly polished aluminum dish. Even with the music playing that sounded loud and alone.

Ohhh, I loved playing "This Little Piggy" with my baby. Her tiny, ticklish feet squirming around. Running my finger right up the middle, her giggle now ringing in my hollow, tortured mind. The strength of her squirming, delightful protest always a marvel as I feel her body growing.

I love the plate Momma made with my Pun'kin's footprint. Don't worry, sweetheart, I'll be home in three months, six days and about three hours.

Focus, Lady, Focus.

Don't worry Sista, I'm taking care of you. Although you lay before me, I can still feel your presence watching me work. Work. My fingers can't touch it, but your energy is all around me.

I wonder if you have babies of your own? My hands tell me you might have been a momma.

Damn, femur is displaced and your hip is shattered. May need someone to help me get those back in place.

Ok, I can do this, complete the inventory. Gotta love good old Army training. Carry on in the midst of total chaos. Physical, mental or both.

Crap, your arm is toast. How many times have I seen this? Right where the body armor ends at the shoulder. Just below the forearm, or what's left.

Tracking the sinews protruding from your tattered arm, harsh bruises from the tourniquet still purple, I can tell you were into CrossFit or something. Your biceps, days later, are still sculpted.

Damn our medics are good, they found your hand. Or perhaps it was one of your buddies who suffered through the blast with you who came upon it somewhere close to the blast? Trying to collect your parts like childhood Easter eggs. I think one of your friends is in here with us as a matter of fact. Either way, I can get your hand fixed up, no worries.

Look at your hands. Nice callouses, but yet still lookin' like a lady, good for you. Tough to have man-looking hands. You didn't.

All your fingers are here, my friend. Nice shade of nail polish, too, like cotton candy.

Such a beautiful hand, and the palm...

There it is, your lifeline. I watch myself trace it till it runs out. It ran out.

I lightly touch my chest making the sign of the Cross. My 122nd soulmate now ready for the next step in her journey. Our journey.

Three months, six days and one hour to go till I can trace your lifeline, Baby.

Hang tough, Pun'kin, your Momma is coming home soon.

There It Is Again

There it is again…

What is that? As hard as I listen, I still can't really tell.

Is it the soft beginning of a laugh? The kind that starts to slowly leak out when a person sees something funny about to happen and thinks "I wouldn't do that if I were you." Or when someone is just starting to guess the punchline of a great joke?

I notice my hands are folded in prayer.

As a matter of fact, my fingers are really clutching each other. Not sure why. Have they been that way for a long time now? No way to tell.

Relaxing, I take the tension out of my knuckles only to realize they're a bit sore. Yesterday was no picnic, no picnic at all.

After three weeks of simulated combat training in the field, the last several days are always extremely taxing. This time was no different.

A tactical night parachute jump from 1,200 feet

in 120 pounds of full combat gear, followed by a 25-mile road march ending with an assault on a simulated enemy village.

The final assault is always such a bitch because you're so smoked from the long road march. My arms always feel like they're going to fall off carrying the M60 machinegun, the "Hog". Perhaps that's why my hands are tight now. Clutching a 16-pound machinegun for 25 miles sucks.

How can you love and hate an inanimate object with such passion? I know every piece of the "Beast" like the back of my hand. I've tried to explain to my civilian friends how my machinegun has a personality, but they have no clue. Like a pig looking at a wristwatch. Old grunts, get it, especially the ones from Vietnam. It was their lifeblood in those jungles.

I always rest the trigger assembly in my pistol belt during long marches to give my arms, back and neck a rest, but if my Squad Leader catches me, it's ass-chewin' time. He's got a point. If we get ambushed and I can't pull the pistol grip out of my Load Bearing Equipment (LBE) immediately, the effectiveness of our most casualty-producing weapon is lost. "Never will I fail my Comrades." Isn't that the main point in the Ranger Creed?

There it is again…

It's only been seconds but that sounded more like a murmur. Not prolonged or painful, but more as if some bad news has just been shared, or you're observing a painful act happening to someone you deeply care about.

I guess we all know that feeling, and those that don't, certainly will.

I vividly remember years ago when my Squad Leader went off to Ranger School leaving me in charge for 58 days. We had a "newbie' in the squad who got news from home his grandpa had passed. It was the first time he had ever known someone who died. It was that kind of murmur.

Difficult to watch a person go through, but ten years of war changes everything. Builds callouses and callouses on your heart, same as those nasty, thick layers of skin covering your hands during a deployment. Both sets of callouses are there for a reason. One clearly seen, the other clearly felt, but not always seen. Those are the tricky ones.

Feeling my palms, the tell-tale signs of the last three weeks are there. Rough, dry, some good deep cracks born of dehydration.

Damn, there it is again.

How can I not know what that is? I've heard it a thousand times and I'm still guessing. Most definitely a cry. Not a cry out, but very soft, very light.

What I don't know is was it happy or sad?

When I returned home from Iraq the first time, it was the middle of the night. Because our unit was in and out of there constantly we didn't have one of those community Welcome Home Yellow Ribbon events like regular units do. We just rolled in, cleaned our gear, accounted for the sensitive items and headed home for a four-day weekend.

Anyway, being the shifty guy that I am, I arranged with my Platoon Leader's wife to grab one of the puppies their dog had had six weeks earlier. I stopped by his house, took about ten minutes to make my selection, and whisked "Bodacious" home. I knew he was the one 'cause as I lay there on the carpet trying to make a selection among the six puppies remaining, he went right after my hands, ears and heart. I loved his attitude from the git-go.

So, "Bo" rode home in my kitbag, amongst all my nasty uniforms and laundry that hadn't been washed in weeks.

It must have been about 0730 when I busted into the apartment. The pre-kindergarten routine was just beginning as I surprised them. My God, what a feeling. Shouting, hugging, kissing the whole works. Then they heard Bo wrestling around in my kitbag. The kids' hands shot straight up in the air like they had just scored an overtime goal. Fingers trembling, grabbing, pulling open the zipper to reveal that yellow ball of fuzz. The giggles and tears of joy really began.

Upstaged by a puppy, go figure. Those three have been thick as thieves ever since.

I think it was that kind of cry, the happy one.

In my line of business when you hear a heartfelt laugh, your mind makes an everlasting impression in order to replay it when the shit gets real. I've had to play scenes like this over and over again. In the darkest of days, over and over again; laughs, joyful cries, puppy breath.

Most of my buddies talk about being able to see everything in the sharpest of colors, but for me, it's the sounds and smells that are sharpest.

There it is again…

Putting those thoughts in their mental cabinet, I lace my hands behind my head and begin to realize how much I love this part of predawn.

I resist the temptation to reach over and press the button on my phone to see what time it is.

This is my time, that's what it is. The time I can truly let my mind drift.

The time the house is still asleep. When the quiet is so quiet you can almost imagine what a deaf person hears. The depth of silence.

But, lying here, knowing we are going to get the word to deploy again, I want to soak up everything. The sounds, the smells, the thoughts. I'd never be able to explain how much this time means to me.

I softly reach over, taking her hand in mine as I listen to my Love dream in the early morning.

Her hand is so soft in mine, not a callous anywhere on her body, heart nor soul. Yes, we've left scars on each other, trying to hurt one another because we didn't know how else to express our love, but those wounds never turned to callouses.

Her hand twitches and squeezes ever so slightly as her dream plays out. I focus, capturing each sound in my mind's ear for the times to come. I'll need them to play over the painful, heart-throbbing crying of lost comrades in arms, my soldiers, my friends, my brothers.

I roll onto my side and take her hand in both of mine and pray. A non-rehearsed prayer asking God to bring us safely back together.

As I finish, the sound of little feet approach the doorway.

"Daddy, can we get into bed with you?"

I throw back the covers as both rascals sneak between us. Bodacious leaps up on the bed and pushes his head under my calloused hand.

All is safe, all is secure.

There it is again…

The sound of true happiness.

The Centurion

The day began as it always did, reaching for a ladle of cool water. Hands aching, large dry cracks stinging as the day welcomed me. My thirst was quenched as freshwater raced down my gullet. Yes, it was still frigid from the lower temperatures of yet another night. It would heat up in no time as the sun, too, promised to torture today.

Many engagements for the Emperor had permanently stained my hands with dirt from numerous countries. Had gouged them, creased them, scarred them, condemned them. But the white callouses in the heart of my palm always took me back to the tender feel of their skin; my wife sensually, my child lovingly. What were they doing now?

Did they know what torment I would deal out this afternoon? For my comrade and I had drawn guard duty on Calvary Hill. We had heard Pilate was sending him, the Sanhedrim sentencing him.

We completed digging holes for the crucifixes last night, three in all. Mars had blessed me with deep sinewy callouses to complete my task. Never a blister, nor second thought, as we prepared the awaiting earth.

My right arm relaxed as the hammer finished pounding the last foot nail into the second thief.

The two criminals were easy, they deserved it. That thought raced through my mind as I adjusted my helmet to see the dust cloud stalking the crowd as it labored along in the mid-morning sun.

I could just see him at the head of the mob, barley shuffling under his burden.

After he was delivered to us we assisted him toward his fate. I felt the dusty sweat under his arm as we hoisted him onto his cross. Crowds, more women than men, cried out, tearing at the rocky earth with their bare hands.

I exerted my entire being as I placed the first cold iron spike in the middle of his soft hand.

Hands so unlike mine, giving, never taking, surrendering with fingers curled, nails encrusted with dirt and blood. The driving clank shattered my soul as it did his bones, the agony in his scream piercing my heart as I handed my partner the hammer.

Is what they say true? Could I be crucifying the living Messiah?

I caressed my tunic to feel the impression of my Eros medallion she had given me before I marched through this God-forsaken desert. A constant reminder we are all subject to God's whims.

Finishing the agonizing task, we pushed the

rough wooden cross towards the sky, the sting of a splinter lodging in my finger. I would learn to cherish this small sliver of wood forevermore.

Easily driving his cross into the ground, for he was lighter than the others, the wood slammed unmercifully into the earth. The snapping of his hands and feet echoing in my mind as I packed dry earth around the base of the cross.

Now the waiting began.

We cast lots for his tunic. It appeared so rough to the eye but yet had been made so soft from the touch and wanting caresses of thousands of lost souls.

The dice tumbled off my fingers and landed in my favor. Winning his tunic, I quickly stored it in my cloak to barter later.

All condemned feel the need to confess or berate; one thief claiming innocence, the other asking this man for forgiveness. He kept silent, sagging onto his nailed broken feet.

I covered my helmeted ears to muffle the constant wailing, for I could see my family in these faithful agonizing faces. Loving, loyal, caring for a man they consider their savior.

Silence suddenly enveloped us all as he began to speak, not with us, but to an unseen,

"My God! My God! Why Have You Forsaken Me?"

"Into your hands, I commend my Spirit."

My aching, well-trained hands grasped my lance to keep the multitudes from rushing forward to hear him.

The earth shook and he was gone. I heard his dying gasp and saw the shiver course through his body. I knew whatever he was here on earth, a carpenter, a king, a soothsayer, was no longer.

The battle-worn lance I clutched, my best friend in many a harsh place took on a life of its own.

I drove the tip into his side, wrists twisting slightly to avoid the rib, ensuring his agony was complete, no more would he suffer.

I could feel his spirit pass through that instrument of death into my soul, like a bolt of lightning, a searing yet refreshing coolness, like no other.

Realizing what I had done, truly done, I withdrew my pike. I saw His flecks of blood covering my stained, now purified hands. He had forgiven me in that moment we were connected.

"Truly, this was the Son of God." I murmured.

I know this. I now believed this truth only after a few short hours in His presence.

I buried my face in my cleansed hands and wept tears of joy and pain knowing He had washed away my transgressions.

My Sandwich

Jesus, Mary and Joseph, I'm hungry. The growling in my stomach and bit of mustard on my right hand both remind me. I tell ya, it won't be sandwiches for dinner tonight. I'm thinking a quick stop at the pub for a celebratory pint and then off to the house for the wife's famous corned beef and cabbage. Or perhaps a bit of boxty?

My lord, I was in the right place at the right time for once, absently crossing myself.

So many of my friends, and thousands upon thousands across the city, are unemployed. I stumble into this job because of my wife's cousin. I suppose lending him a hand when he got off the boat at Ellis paid its dues.

It's the right thing to do, giving a man a hand up. It happens here in this cesspool of a city but most often people are just stomping on each other to try and get ahead.

I absently pat my protesting stomach again knowing there is one last task to complete and then she's all done. She's ALL DONE. I still can't believe we came together to complete this project in record time.

My mind takes a slight detour as I think on the blokes working this job. For the most part, they've become close mates. Coming from all over the world, meeting on this one jobsite, joining arms on one monumental opportunity. We may not go down in history by name, but by God, people will look at what we've done here and think the hand of the Lord Himself reached down and blessed our project with divine intervention. What a triumph! At a time our country could surely use one.

I can feel my Dad's hand upon my shoulders as we come to an end. The sun's rays starting to slowly draw shadows on our city. To think, the 22-year-old son of an ironworker from the docks of Limerick to be the last human up here at this time, on this project. Watching the city breathe as the immortal sun blesses the day.

All because my daft boss whacked the hell out of his fingers yesterday while trying to secure a stubborn rivet. His loss, not mine. Most everyone else is so tired, they gladly told me to tighten down the last nuts and call it a day.

Call it a project. Call it history.

But alas, like my grandfather and his grandfather before him, perhaps I have a bit of James Joyce in me? No more apparent was this than the first time I was sent home by the priests at Sacred Heart for a poem I had written proclaiming the

Dead Rabbits Gang was the reason the city had changed and not the Civil War. I claimed to be the American James Joyce! Father Ian didn't appreciate the analogy. I can still feel Mum's fingers piercing my earlobe, almost pulling it off my head, while I got the speech.

"How can you ever compare street thugs to the valiant men who fought in the War? Are you turning into a Hooligan? Is there a Hooligan sitting here at my table? Defaming the most creative modern-day writer known to man? And a fellow countryman at that!"

"Hold your hand out! I'm going to whack your knuckles harder than the soft Fathers did. I will."

How proud would Mother be? Right now? Knowing at this very moment her Ironworker-Poet was taking in the last sunset God would paint on this city before a modern-day landmark would become history?

I inwardly chuckled knowing her stubborn Irish pride wouldn't allow her to congratulate me. Lord have mercy on her friends! They'd be hearing about this for months, no, years, to come. A good bit of the storytelling art not having been lost on her side of the family either.

"Auch Biddy, my God, you should have seen the Boy! Standing there, the last one on the project, he was. Just like Gabriel standing ready to do battle with the Lion! Chest puffed out, looking all high and mighty, wrench in one hand, lunch pail in the other, claiming he had just slayed the largest project known to man," she would say.

"And what's the wee man gonna do? Pull out a slab of corned beef and whack the lion with it? Or perhaps he'd be better served by clutching that stale piece of bread like a sword and using that? For I'm certain his good-for-nothing charlatan of a wife packed my precious boy stale bread in his tin. The crust no doubt! Never should have married her at such a young age. Youngest daughter of a tinker is my guess."

Ahhh, yes, the whole time she'd have not taken a breath. Almost an art form with her hands flailing about in the air, fingers pointing at the ladies in the coop, all nodding silently, waiting a turn to chirp into the growing mayhem.

Mother's a beauty, no doubt, she's a beauty. And right about the stale bread. I'd take it right now, I would.

I can't believe I dropped my sandwich at lunch. Bouncing and bouncing till I couldn't see the damn thing. Bread going one way, beef in the other, like they'd spent too much time together and couldn't wait to be separated. Seriously, my fingers fumbling, snatching, grabbing, and there it went. Floating to freedom. Dumb bastard.

Reaching down into my tool bag, my fingers find the wrench I need. Amazing how few tools our crew lost after 400 some odd days on the job. You could count 'em on one hand. Any tool we dropped at this height would sure as hell make a dent in whatever it landed on.

Except my sandwich, the pigeons would snag it out of mid-air.

Nothing like sitting astride an iron beam a thousand feet in the air. Lines taut, buckles straining. What a life!

Better focus and get these nuts tightened down before the 404th sun sets on our project.

I can tighten three, slide over and tighten the next set. Won't have to move the scaffolding, which is a major pain in the arse. Wish I had a nickel for each time we moved it. I'd be a rich man.

What I do know, is when my hands pull the wrench tightening the final nut, I can tell everyone at the pub, my family, friends and everyone else who'll listen, I was the last man to officially work on the structure of this 1,494-foot historic landmark.

"Look, Ma," I'll say. "Every time you stare up at that glorious spike, the lightning rod, you'll know your boy tightened the last bolts completing that modern-day piece of art. The last bolts, by God!"

Then, at that very moment, I'll share my quest for infamy, a true piece of history itself, only to be seen by the privileged few. Mother will admonish me; then quickly realize the legend I had created.

As I gathered the last of my tools, the flat tip on my favorite screwdriver winked at me in the waning sun. Beckoning me, taunting me to etch my poem into the very steel crowning the city.

As the good Lord was my only witness He saw my hands scrape, etch, and shave my soul into the steel plate holding up the lightning rod.

My task complete with cramped and bloody fingers, I dusted off the bits of metal shavings. In my best rendition of James Joyce, my thick Irish brogue proclaimed to the swirling wind and sunset...

"My hands pulled
While the last of the day's sun shone off the nut and wrench
Still joined
Afraid, not wanting to part
But parting nonetheless
Iron tears shed
Upon massive structure
Crowning peak yearning to collect
The bolts of God Himself
In tortured day
Or sleepless City night"

With an epic verse scrawled into its skin, I alone can now proclaim the Empire State Building is complete.

I Love Tuesdays

I *loooovvvve* Tuesdays. It's not just the fact that Monday's over, which is never a lot of fun in anyone's mind, but now the real week begins.

Refocusing my thoughts, I watch my fingertip skim across the page of my new novel for English class.

Tuesdays and reading are the two things I really love. I do, I do, I do! This year, like many others, the characters in my books (and life) will quickly come into my life and then leave. Only to be drawn back in at my beckoning with a short trip to the library. They make my life different in so many ways but then casually depart with the turning of a page or closing of a cover. Not to say they haven't taken up permanent residence in my mind, 'cause they have. A whole family of characters always chiming in on my thoughts and personal conversations. A British accent here, a French one there, and one of my favorites is the old Bostonian. I don't get to make many choices in my life but choosing what each character sounds and looks like is mine, and mine alone. Cool thing is, no one will ever know what my new friends sound like inside my head. Only me.

There are permanent voices in my life I don't get to choose, that's for sure. Most mornings Mom's wake up shout pierces my solitude like the first sawing stroke of a beginning violinist. Forcefully *eeeeking* its way into the graceful symphony playing in my mind. Mom's voice makes a daily impression just like Anne Frank, Romeo and Juliet, or Silas Marner, all trying to change my life, some succeeding, some not. The majority don't have the courage to stick around when issues really come up. I don't count on any of them.

Bumping along on Tuesday's bus ride I use my chipped fingernail to scratch a hole in the frost so I can watch the world slip past. Yesterday couldn't have gone fast enough. It's like everyone was bound and determined to be sour. I'm a Tuesday gal, no doubt. Everyone is a bit upbeat, having accepted the fact the weekend is officially over.

"F'N Monday" is the favorite term around the house. It kinda stalls at first, dripping by, like the bad faucet in the kitchen. Drip, drip, drip.

Monday night arrives, puts on the brakes, slows drastically as we figure out how to stay out of the way. A few hours later the tempo picks up, the TV blares, we're forgotten, and Tuesday's homework demands my attention. I silently creep off at the appointed time sliding the bedroom door shut.

Our bed welcomes me (if I get there first) and my Tuesday cautiously tiptoes toward the calendar. Now it's time to greet whatever friends I'm entertaining that evening. Slipping under the sheets I click on the flashlight, my fingers making funny animal shadows, all the while welcoming a new world.

On occasion, Monday refuses to give up its time with me when my finger pushes the little red sliding thing forward and the light doesn't come on. This failure ushers in frustration and the resounding feeling of guilt knowing I'm going to have to find a place to get some more batteries.

Last week it was the drug store three blocks away. I waited in the back till the pharmacist wasn't looking and slid two packs deep into my greedy pockets. Good thing about winter's arrival, I guess, is I can hide stuff in my big coat. Not my favorite thing to do, but like Anne Frank, you gotta do what you gotta do.

My best caper so far was the "Great Flashlight Robbery". There wouldn't have been one if Gravel Voice hadn't caught me reading one Sunday night. He saw the shadows under my sheets, ripped the covers back, screamed at me in some language brought on by Sunday Night Football and beer, snatched my silver friend out of my hand and KAPLOOOIE! My flashlight met its destiny against the bedroom wall turning into a thousand pieces. Never to shine again.

But anyways, the next morning, Drip Drop Monday, I noticed Gravel Voice left his truck unlocked. Every adult in the house was decked out in some form of unconsciousness so the coast was clear. I hoisted the lid on his tool box casually sitting on the back seat. There it was! The Holy Grail of flashlights. Man, what a beauty! Long heavy black handled jobbie. Not the slick shiny silver one like I had become close friends with, but the kind that holds three D cell batteries! One twist of my wrist and it was like the Piggly Wiggly parking lot when the big lights come on. I could hardly contain myself as I quickly slid it into my backpack and headed for the bus stop.

"Blackie" became a critical part of my education, only sneaking him out when the voices, smells and music subsided. No way I can get caught using it, I'd be in huge trouble.

I've got the best hiding place for it, too. One of the wall boards at the end of the bed came loose, and with a bit of coaxing, and a few splinters in my fingertips, I pulled the siding back, yanked out that pink stuff and slid it right in the wall. Perfect hiding spot.

Old Gravel Voice never knew where it went. Not sure where he went either. Two months later doofus was gone. He should have known stealing stuff out of everyone's purses and wallets is a party foul. Especially in Mom's crowd.

Alas, he was soon replaced by another loser. I love the word "Alas". My fingers retrace it every time it appears. Not sure why, but I think it's the way it sounds in my mind. Kinda like a sigh of resignation but one ending with some hope. Not giving up but giving in without an end truly in sight.

"Alas, Gravel Voice smashed my flashlight, but I stole his while he was passed out sleeping off a bender." I can see my English friends using it, too. As a matter of fact, I think I've read it several times in Shakespeare, who has now drifted into my life.

The *sssssshhhhhh* of the bus air brakes brings me back to reality. Carefully marking the page in *Hamlet*, I gently shake my little brother's knee to wake him up. He's just learning the pleasure of books, a world all his own. I've tried to spend as much time as I can getting him interested. I pray he does, it's the only way out. Especially for a shy kid like him.

His tiny warm hand interlaces with mine as all of us pile off the bus on this glorious Tuesday.

At the age of six he doesn't have to endure the Drip Drop Mondays like I do. He gets to stay at home with the crowd, trying to be as invisible as he can. Just like I used to. He's become quite good at it, just like waving a hand over his face, he disappears like he's wearing Harry Potter's invisibility cloak.

He loves when I read him Harry Potter. My reading world takes me in a different direction now, but this is a love we can share together. Seeing his eyes light up is truly magical to me.

We tumble off the bus with the other kids and

quickly walk into school. He squeezes my hand, tugging my arm a bit towards his favorite room, ensuring I know not to miss the turn toward the cafeteria.

I smile back at him, "I know the feeling, Buddy, we'll be there in a minute."

Yes, the empty feeling of not having eaten since Saturday night when leftover pizza becomes a treat. I can still feel the hot breakfast tray in my hands every morning I got to come to school. Just like him, I'd eat so fast I would almost throw up. Left me with hiccups all morning. I wasn't the only one.

Alas, you learn to cope with the weekends, praying for school to arrive, getting to eat with your friends.

I nod my head and his hand slips out of mine as he bolts for the breakfast line.

My goodness, I love that kid.

And Tuesdays

And reading

And eating

Alas, I hate crack

And heroin

And alcohol

And a mother who can't stay straight.

Just like Anne Frank, maybe I can protect my little guy, keeping him under my wing. 'Till we can fly on our own. Away from the drugs, the trailer, and guys like Gravel Voice.

I love Tuesdays.

Hand Wringer

Wringing my hands, wringing my hands. Thank God I'm not a professional poker player. I'd never win any money. But then again, it's a tell I've almost learned to rid myself of.

Momma never wrung her hands.

Damn, she was a nail biter. Right down to the quick. I'd look at her poor tormented fingers and wonder how many hours she'd gnawed each and every nail. Working them to the point where there was nothing physically left to bite off. It looked so painful. But *merci*, the pain never stopped her.

My guess is the alcohol began with the closing of the mine. Daddy never drank much before that fateful time. Maybe a social beer after the union meetings, never in the house, though. At least not when we were awake.

As a young wife, Momma wouldn't allow it. However, she had no choice in the years to come. The hours she spent gnawing her fingernails were probably the exact amount of time Daddy and his workmates were at the company bar hammering those 25¢ beers. All his buddies who'd elected to take part in the wildcat strike were there hammering the beers, the union and the company. It was in their nature, had to hammer and pick away at something till the sunshine came peeping through.

Union leaders said the families needed more support. Daddy believed it. I can still remember him pounding the supper table with his coal black fist, getting his point across to a woman who most definitely was on his side. We just sat there and flinched every time his ham-like fist shook the table. Thanking God it was the table taking the beating instead of us.

Stop the hand wringing. The skin on my knuckles is worn smooth by this incessant habit.

The hands next to mine are as cold as ice. Fingers laced together, not moving. If I were in his chair, mine would be drumming, fidgeting, picking…who knows what? Nope, his were as still as the surface of the quarry lake on a summer's morning.

I miss our small quarry lake in West Virginia where we swam every chance we could. The water so clear and warm for the first six feet and then frigid and dark as the depths of a coal mine. We had such a blast as kids camping, drinking, making out by our quarry. Then Johnson got so drunk he drove his Mustang off our favorite diving cliff, slowly sinking to the bottom. Past the warmth of the sun to the depths of the earth. No one wanted to swim there afterward, thinking his body would come floating up right next to you. Johnson never did get out of the car. I wonder if today's teenagers even know his tragic story? Or has it become urban legend?

As we waited, I scratched my immaculately groomed hair. All the gel now forming a cast upon my skull. Gotta keep up those appearances, extremely important in my profession. My mentors drilled constantly on this. Color of the tie, custom suits, manicured nails, the whole shebang. "And for gawd's sake, work on that hillbilly accent!"

My signature look? Solid gold cufflinks Momma had made for my graduation. She had Daddy's only two pieces of gold jewelry, his wedding ring and crucifix, along with Papaw's watch fob, all melted down. A friend of the family handcrafted the gold into perfect ovals with small crucifixes adorning the top of each one. I still remember what Momma said as I opened the gift.

"You'll need these in your new line of business, son. Daddy would be so proud of you. The cross will keep the good Lord Jesus in your thoughts."

The memories of my two favorite alcoholic coal miners are melted into my cufflinks. Both always accompanied me in this moment. Both men tormented Momma down to the quick. Down to the very bone.

I solidly placed my hand on my client's fore-arm, squeezing re-assuredly.

"Won't be long now. I can feel it."

His look changed not a bit. Not even a slight twitch in his arm. This one was cold-hearted. I could feel the darkness of his soul emanating from his core as though I was sitting next to some type of carnivore who only acted on pure visceral instinct. A chill ran through my being.

I couldn't let the gravity of the moment pull me in. Stay cool. Following my training, I crossed my legs, smoothed out the crease in my trousers, and folded my hands on my knees, projecting the consummate, confident professional. No one would ever know my gut was wrenching a mile a minute.

I know tonight's news cycle will shout the judgment, regardless of the outcome. The head-lines cloaking the human next to me, drawing me in, critically hammering, clawing at my skills, my performance, my professional reputation. All of these are always up for grabs depending on the news source you favor.

The small-town coffee house chatter will surround me and those I love. I've heard it so many times before, yet I always listen. Although I can't show it, I do have my own very personal opinion. I can never share my real thoughts with even my closest family and friends.

"How could that son of a bitch defend a man like that? The bastard was holding the dripping-hammer when the cops showed up. Wife lying on the kitchen floor, beaten to a pulp, beyond recognition! Him and his fancy lawyer need to burn in Hell!"

How many times had my father come close to this damming act? All tanked up, clutching the porch railing with both hands, not even in the door yet and there stood Momma, nails bleeding, clutching the Good Book, hammering away about God, us kids, and wrecking the family.

His fingers never tightened around the smooth handle of any clawhammer the way my client's had. Honestly, there are only three folks in the world who know the facts. Him, me and, of course, his dearly departed wife.

Did that matter anymore? The law winding itself around so many axles? God granted me the gift, the mental clarity and articulation skills to wind, unwind and wind yet again, until a jury of everyday citizens doing their civic duty had no way of possibly untying the knots I had skillfully created.

Hell, yea, I could create reasonable doubt!

It was my gift, but you'd have to ask the Lord or the Devil who granted it. Lying in my bed deep in the night, I surely couldn't tell you.

Sixteen capital cases to my credit. Twelve murdering sons of bitches walking the streets today would testify I have a God-given gift. Sixteen lives

ended, families crushed and the communities im-
pacted would all say the Devil had spawned my
gift. My clients and I know their dirty little secrets.

The courtroom's energy quickly shifted as the
bailiff led the jury back to their seats.

I spun my wedding ring, I wrung my hands.

My client and I stood as beckoned.

"Ladies and gentlemen, what say you in the
Capital trial of the State of West Virginia vs. Ian
McDonagal for manslaughter in the first degree?"

Ohhh Momma, please help me stop wringing
my hands.

The jury's spokesperson stood and pulled out
a wrinkled piece of paper.

Quiet your hands. Quiet your hands.

Her face tells me their verdict before her lips
begin to move. Would Momma and Daddy be
proud right now?

Lord save us all.

Her Day

It's just another *Manic Monday.*

Man, the Bangles got that right. My fingers, with their freshly painted nails, reach out and turn off the radio.

One last sip of coffee, a quick prayer and then I can head on in. Does the weekend have to end? What a fantastic few days.

I treasure my birthday above all other holidays except Christmas. The Lord gets that one. Nothing beats a summer birthday, particularly when you get pampered all week by your family. Gorgeous pair of earrings to boot!.

Tugging my earlobe and glancing in the rear-view mirror I see the encrusted emeralds. They capture the sunlight and fill the car with little beams of green. How beautiful.

All righty, "Lord, give me the strength to help my kiddos. May your light shine through me giving them the courage to change, break their cycle, and become the persons you know they can be. In your name I pray. Amen."

Crunch, crunch, crunch across the parking lot. Always reminds me of being back on the farm.

Strolling to my end of the corridor, I'm struck by how abandoned it seems. No one at my end. Not even the creepy janitor.

Buses are right on time. I hear their tires chewing on the gravel.

Ok, there's the herd-like sound of 150, ill-adjusted kids shuffling in. The quiet buzz heightens as their government breakfast kicks in.

All right, there's the first reprimand of the day, as a behavioral specialist guides his crew past the intersection just down the hallway.

Muffled silence resumes as the classroom doors shut giving me 20 minutes before my first appointment.

Who's my 8:30?

Snap, he's a tough one. I'll see if I can get him to talk today. I've had to turn his drug-infested mother into Child Advocacy twice for the bruises she's made him wear to school. Really lady? Can't pick out a clean shirt to wear instead of a knot below his eye?

There are times, I can't decide if I love my job or hate my job.

I tuck my hair behind my ears, check my makeup and head down the vacant hallway to his room.

Oops, there he is. Hiding in the back, head down, being invisible.

I lightly tap the glass in the classroom door.

He looks up, making eye contact and I beckon him with a quick curl of my fingers.

What? Was that a smile? Better not get my hopes up.

"Good morning, kind sir."

Not a head bob, nor "Hey", "Hi", or "Yo". Nada. Must've been a tough weekend, poor kid.

"All righty, I see how it's going to be this morning, so why don't I just talk? Will that work for you?" We both settle into our chairs for the stare down. Instead of his voice, I hear a metallic clicking sound.

What was that? Why's the back door opening? That's odd. A shadow passing my door window catches my attention.

Jesus help us. I think he was carrying a gun.

My God, he is.

My training takes over, I grab the door handle, lock it, and pull my kiddo behind the desk.

Sweet Jesus, my heart is beating so loud I can't hear anything.

Did that man even see us?

No sounds... I grab my purse fumbling for my cellphone.

My trembling fingers dial 911.

"911, What is your emergency?"

How can she be so calm?

"Someone's in our school and I think he's got a gun."

"Where are you located, Ma'am?"

"The alternative school on Johnsonville Road."

I slowly lift my index finger signaling "*Ssssshhhh*". My God, my kiddo looks calm. Can't he see how terrified I am?

I sense the shadow close to our door again.

Slowly crowding us further under the desk, I push my phone into the folds of my blouse.

Gently grabbing my kiddo's head I slowly bring it as close to my face as I can.

"Someone is in the building with a gun." I stop, almost panting.

"We stay under this desk and don't say a peep."

Like he would anyway, right?

He slowly nods, understanding me.

Has time stopped?

He barely breaths, "I won't."

My heart shatters into a million pieces. His first spoken words to me are wrapped in this tragedy. I'd almost forgotten what his voice sounds like.

My Lord, I love these kids.

The shadow is near again, I can feel him.

Son of a bitch knew where to come into the school so he wouldn't be seen.

The door handle is moving!

It's clicking!

Kiddo's arms tighten around me.

Neither of us is breathing.

My heart's in my throat.

The shadow is at the door.

It's locked, it's locked.

The handle's jiggling.

In pure silence I look into my kiddo's eyes and tell him it's going to be okay.

His deep brown eyes understand, he knows we are going to make it.

My phone chirps.

"Help is on the way. Do not move, Ma'am, unless you can escape safely. Stay on the line, we are with you, it's going to be okay."

Does anyone else know he's in here?

The Shadow's footsteps start down the hallway towards the cafeteria.

That son of a bitch, he's not doing this to my kids!

I quickly get back into my purse and feel the handle of the 9mm pistol my father gave me two years ago. God bless him for making me take those classes. "Never know when you're going to need it, Honey." His favorite words at the firing range.

In a raspy hush, I breathe my plan. "It's going to be okay. I am going to open our door, and on the count of three we're going to run outside and hide by the vans until the police arrive."

"I will," he softly croaks. "Are you staying with me?"

"No, Honey, I have to take care of this guy."

"ONE, TWO, THREE!" Grabbing his arm, I bolt into the hallway.

Back door swinging open, I push him outside,

knowing I could feel the bee sting of a bullet at any moment.

He's safe. He's running to the vans.

I quickly turn on the step grabbing the back-door handle and go into the hallway.

Crouching against the wall, I slowly creep towards the cafeteria.

"Where are you, you bastard?" I breathe aloud.

His shadow crosses the intersection of the hallway as he hears me.

I can hear the sirens, the cops are on the way, *thank* God.

Some type of barrel pokes around the corner announcing the Shadow.

Thanks for the warning, you dumb bastard.

Come on, come on….

There you are.

He appears in the hallway carrying some type of shotgun.

My training takes over.

Breathe.

Locate the red dot.

Aim.

Squeeze. Squeeze. Squeeze.

The deafening cracks of my 9mm fill the hallway.

The Shadow is falling, I hit him, he's falling.

His eyes find mine.

I know those eyes. He was here. He was one of my kids.

His finger jerks as he hits the ground and his shotgun fires harmlessly, peppering the picture-covered wall.

His eyes blink twice, then roll lifelessly to the ceiling.

I bolt for the back door slamming it open.

I'm alive!

I'm running.

Stumbling to the vans, I see my kiddo hiding near the back tires.

"We're safe, we're safe," I blurt out.

He hugs me closely as my pistol falls to the ground.

"It's going to be okay," he whispers.

"We are going to be okay."

His Day

"I don't give a damn if you say anything now or ever, you little shit. Now get your ass in the van."

I felt the back of her hand before the last word ever left her mouth, that bitch.

Thank God she pawned her ring right after the divorce or I'd be wearing the mark of her pathetic little pebble on my check.

Given the amount of times she's slapped me around, I could probably tell you every bump she has in her boney scarred hands. I hate that bitch, I can't wait till she's dead. Meth-head, crack whore, who did I piss off to have to call her Mom?

There it is, the white van lumbering up to my stop. That thing's a piece of shit, too. Driver's not a bad dude, though. Except for all the stupid rings he wears. What's up with that? You'd think they'd screen these people.

The side of the van says I'm precious cargo? Really? Precious to whom? This fuck-tard with a skull ring on each finger, and two rings in his nose? What crack house did he wake up in this morning, anyway?

Silence. My weapon of choice today. Always effective, and quite frankly, I'm pretty sure it's what landed me at this prison-like little turd of a school program. Took me two full weeks of not saying a word to anyone in sixth grade, bouts with the junior high counselor, then the high school counselor, next the vice principal, what a shit stain that lady is, and finally the big dog. The principal himself. Actually, a pretty cool guy, played college football.

Holy crap he's big, almost broke my silence when he put his meat hook on my shoulder and squeezed. Not so much because it hurt, but just enough to let me know he wasn't giving up on me. Kinda like he was onto my game.

Didn't let him in, though. Just sat on my hands, looked down and said, "*zeeeeroooooo.*" Winning me six months in this van, having to spend time with the other boneheads in this stupid ass program.

Really? Do they actually think I'm going to say anything to these other delinquents stuck in the same situation I am? At least I know I'm intelligent, these other idiots are brain dead. I swear you can smell the leftover dope on their clothes as they climb into our custom Uber.

I do have to say one kid is a total nut job. Not the drug type, just a freaking psycho. He needs to go to the next level of whatever this education program is called. He's whacked.

Ahh yes, here we are, the abandoned grade school. Shuffle through the gravel parking lot to get chow.

Mouth shut, I stretched out my hands grabbing the tray full of the best food our government can offer, then head off to my corner to inspect my plate. Scarf it down, say nothing, move to the day's "Bitch Session".

Bitch session. I love my first class. A full half-hour of these other toads spewing their problems and whining about how bad off they are. Really? Is this supposed to be helping anyone?

Staring at my laced fingers, I watch them twitch as I recite my times tables in my head. Gotta do something.

The counselor asks me if I have anything to share. My silence confirms I detest sharing anything with this group of idiots.

Yes! It's over. Finally.

Me? My mind screams as she motions to me indicating it's my turn to join her for our half-hour of private nothingness.

I choose to say nothing to you again, but actually, I am listening to what you're saying, 'cause some of it makes sense about my shitty-ass life; resentment, drug addiction, and breaking the poverty cycle.

Who the hell was that?

I see her head flinch, too, as a shadow slips

past the door.

I saw him.

Weird, no one comes in the backdoor.

What's she doing locking us in here?

I watch her hand dart for her purse. Damn big bag.

Hey, we're talking here Lady. Put your phone away.

What the fuck is she doing?

"911, What is your emergency." I can hear through her phone.

Her rasping whisper sends goosebumps from my head to my toes.

"Someone's in our school and I think he's got a gun."

"Where are you located, Ma'am?"

"The alternative school on Johnsonville road."

Her fingertips pressed to her lips say "*Sssshh*".

I sense a shadow close to our door.

Her soft hand and arm brush me back behind her desk. Her hand's shaking, holding the phone.

That's neat, she has on new earrings. Those are pretty cool. Love the green stones.

Grabbing my head and bringing it so close to her face I can feel and smell her coffee breath. She barely whispers to me.

"Someone's in the building with a gun." She stops, to take two quick breaths. "We're staying under this desk, and don't say a peep."

Me? Say a peep? Really? How long have you

known me? Four months? Have I said more than two words to you?

I slowly nod my head.

I feel the concern on my cheeks as her warm hands cradle them.

She quickly smiles. A smile etched into my memory forever. It was the first genuine smile I was ever given, showing someone truly cared about me. I felt it as much as I saw it. My God it was nice.

The look of pride on her face when I uttered "I won't." spoke volumes at that very moment, of what she thought I could be.

The Shadow was passing again.

Jesus, I thought, we are at the very back corner of the school. No one ever comes down to this end of the hallway unless they have an appointment.

The door handle is moving! The door handle is clicking!

Our arms tighten around each other as we collectively stop breathing. I can only hear the drumbeat of my heart inside my exploding head.

He's pushing on the door. It's locked, it's locked, it's locked. The handle's jiggling.

She slowly turns my head and looks into my eyes. They say we are going to be okay. I believe them, so deep green with little sparkles. We are going to be okay.

Her phone chirps. "Help is on the way. Do not move, Ma'am, unless you can escape safely. Stay on the line, we are with you, it's going to be okay."

Does anyone else know he's in here?

I hear the Shadow's footsteps start down the hallway towards the cafeteria.

What is she doing? Why is she pulling a gun out of her purse?

"It's going to be okay. On the count of three, I am going to unlock the door and we are running outside. We'll hide by the vans till the police arrive."

"I will," croaks out of my mouth. "Are you staying with me?"

"No, Honey, I have to take care of this guy."

"ONE, TWO, THREE!" Her hand clasps my arm as we bolt into the hallway.

Backdoor swinging open, I feel the sun and heat blanket me as I sprint toward the vans.

I skid under the van and watch in horror as she goes back into the building.

Three loud shots ring out. Then one different one!

Flashes in the hallway. Sirens close. Police cars.

There she is! She's running outside, she's running! She sees me by the van tires.

"We're safe, we're safe."

I grab her tightly, my fingers lacing behind her back squeezing.

"It's going to be okay," I whisper in her ear as her pistol falls to the ground. "We are going to be okay."

The Day's Shadow

It's like the surface of the moon. Every time I look at it that's what I think. Distinct craters, peaks, valleys, small pocked areas becoming lakes when water is present. But there isn't. Not today.

The palm of my hand won't become a lake today. The craters, peaks and valleys are the landscape of a dark reminder of when the asshole held my palm to the stovetop. Was busting in on him and my Mom worthy of a lifelong brand only the devil could have drawn?

I learned a valuable lesson. Pain gets your way. Short and sweet, always does.

To this day, any son of a bitch not heeling to my will earns my wrath. I can feel and almost see the point of no return approaching, just like a finish line in an elementary school foot race.

I experienced my rage a few weeks after my hand healed and the doctor took the bandage off. I was living with Grandma until the child advocacy folks got done with their investigation. She had two boys next door who were brothers, a few years older than me, but they were assholes. No doubt.

"Hey, dude, nice hand, looks like hamburger," they taunted.

"Your momma catch you playin' with your-self?"

I attacked the smaller one and couldn't stop. The nerves in my palm screaming out as my hand balled into a fist. The first swing unleashed years of torment. The intimate feel of his nose crunching beneath my fists stood still in time. Like I was watching a movie and paused the frame. What a liberating feeling.

The rest of the fight was a blur. His brother jumped me from behind and I quickly threw him to the ground and wrapped my fingers tightly around his throat to the point I could feel his heart beating. First time I got to see someone turn blue. Looked like a bruised blueberry at the bottom of your cereal bowl.

Destiny slyly revealed herself at that exact mo-ment. She was a traffic cop standing with her white-gloved hands briskly waving me toward an endless roundabout of shadows, broken street-lights and constant darkness. I gladly jumped into her flow of traffic relieved not to have to guess my fate anymore.

My darkness isn't totally dark. It's not the pitch black which breaks when your hand strikes a match and all you can see is the burning tip of your illuminated fingers coupled with the flaming matchhead.

No, not the total darkness of death, either, which I think of often. I dream and feel the depth of that darkness. More complete.

It's a darkness that is too hard to read in. Creating short thick shadows marking the presence of anything with a frame but not revealing the object.

Oh, but now I know who and what those objects are. Destiny shed a new splinter of light for me ever so quickly. Her instrument is resting here in my hands. Cool and handsome in its destructiveness.

Once seen, it will demand complete respect.

Stroking the metal barrel and wooden stock I see its scars. Especially the wood. The nicks and dents in the grain tell its story. Like my scarred hands it can cause blunt trauma alone but chooses to act as part of the larger body to fulfill the collective goal. The wood, when acting in chorus with the metals and plastic, can cause massive destruction.

Yes, its scars tell a journey, don't they? "No scars, no proof," is what Grandpa used to say. Where it's been, what it's been party to, how on occasion it's part of the destructive whole; capable of putting sustenance on the table, while also capable of taking what some would call precious life.

Life? Fuck life.

It's been a constant dull headache in my tormented mind. A smoldering ember eventually burning down an entire forest. An unseen festering cut, eventually causing gangrene and robbing something precious from you.

Life? Yea, fuck that.

Who took me to this point? I know exactly who made me believe I was lower than a piece of whale shit.

I can still see his hairy hands and forearms holding my hand to the stovetop as the red searing circles devoured my flesh like a starving animal. I can't shake the smell.

Oh, I know who you are.

Now, I know where you are. Fucker.

This very morning my friend and I are coming to get you. Right back to where I spent six months of my life. Strange thing is, the place you are hiding, or working, brought me some comfort. For a time anyway.

The folks working there helped me start to illuminate the darkness. Helped too much almost. Just as I started to figure it out, they graduated me and sent me back to the endless roundabout of high school shadows. The dark shroud slipping firmly back into place.

I'll be careful, it's not those folks I'm after.

It's the old son of a bitch pushing the broom down your hallways. No doubt whispering damaging shit to the kids there to get help.

Right after my scarred forefinger releases fury upon your ass, sending you to hell, I'm heading right to the cafeteria for your girlfriend. Nothing personal, Mother, but you were the main cause of my charade.

Go ahead, hand out the government breakfast tray to the kids who can't protect themselves.

I'll protect them by putting your forever dammed soul to rest. A dark tortured rest if I can help it. You bitch.

OK, there's the third white van crunching across the gravel to its parking spot.

My palm begins tingling as my fingertips gently turn off my truck's ignition.

Who's the woman going in the back door? She looks familiar to me.

There he is.

Fucker's smoking a cigarette, not knowing it's his last. Off he goes, back inside.

Time check, 8:30. Kids are done with breakfast and heading to class.

I've checked and rechecked the number of shells in my shotgun, but for some reason my finger pushes the ejection port to check again.

"Time to make things right, time to make things right," drums in my head as I walk through the parking lot to the backdoor. The door gently gives way, making no real noise.

Breath. Walk softly.

Past the first counselor's room and down to the end of the hallway.

Wait. Was there someone in that room?

I slowly retraced my steps back to the first office.

Why would anyone have an office at this end of the school, anyway?

Nope, no one's in there. Door's locked.

Back down the hallway. Take a left toward the janitor's room.

I bet that fucker's in there, just hanging out.

I think I heard a door. The backdoor I just came in!

I turn the corner and there she is.

It's her, my first counselor...

No! Wait! You know me!

You know what they did!

What are you aiming at me!

She's aiming at me... three sounds, three stings...

I'm falling...

My shotgun barks, ripping all the kid's pictures off the wall.

No, please, wait... I haven't completed my destiny.

I haven't righted my wrongs.

They are still breathing, they are still living.

My scarred hand tingles on the cool tile.

I see the shadows.

It's my shadow. It's come to meet me.

Heart and Sole

The ring of keys dangled in my hand as it had done so many times before, making the soft musical sound in rhythm with my echoing footsteps. My fingers intimately knowing the feel of each key for each door. So many years I've done this dance in the dawn of a new day or by the soft glow of the emergency exit sign. The cherished solitude of these moments forever stored in the lockbox of my heart. Not a soul can pry those memories from me. I alone hold the key.

I can remember us as young kids hiding from my father as he started his rounds. He knew we had stashed ourselves in corners or behind some of the larger workstations, holding our breath as his footsteps grew louder. The musical pace of the keys picking up as he hunted us down.

Unlike myself, he was a bouncer. He'd bounce the ring of keys in the air from one hand to another like a hot potato waiting to burn his palms. *Ching.....Ching...Ching...*

"Shhhh, he's getting closer." I'd whisper to my younger brothers and sisters as he approached. I'd always have to press my hand over my youngest sister's mouth to hold in the giggling. "Blaba Girdy", my goodness, even as an adult she couldn't keep anything in. I miss the musical staccato of her giggle. *Ching...Ching...Ching...Ching.*

"AHHH HHAAA!" Dad would yell as he discovered our hideout, making us all scream and bolt to the next hole in the wall. We always had to keep in front of his routine, so we didn't get locked in. Not sure how he did it but he always found us.

He always found us, especially when we most needed him to. Even as adults when we were hiding from hard decisions or a failing relationship. This fact became most apparent to me when my middle brother returned from Vietnam. He arrived home to a small family party, dinner really, and then disappeared for three days. We searched high and low for him, every dive we could think of, the VFW, American Legion, the old Dutch Creek Mine. As a veteran himself, Dad knew where he was. Maybe not physically, but mentally he knew. He might have known all along, too; the solitude was what my brother sought.

Dad found him. Where? He never told us, but we could tell they shared a coveted bond now. My father was born in the Battle of the Bulge and my brother in the jungles of Vietnam. My brother remarked when Pops found him that weekend he knew he was safe as the musical sound of the keys being bounced from hand to hand approached his hiding place. *Ching....Ching....Ching...Ching.*

"Son, it's time to come home," is all Pops said.

What would my father say now, after handing me the keys so many years ago? I've prayed and prayed over my decision and I'd like to think in some small way he gave me insight from the grave, helping me to this point.

Lord knows, every single person I've talked to has tried to weigh in on this decision. We've held family meeting after family meeting to see if we could reach a consensus. Time after time, with many hard-fought debates and arguments, often getting emotional to the point of fistfights, all five kids would raise a hand to vote and no clear majority ever became apparent. One of us would be thinking something different. Girdy got so emotional one time she slapped me across the cheek, leaving four beautifully sculpted fingerprints. She blamed me until the day of her death, like most local folk do.

I can hear conversations stop or reduce to whispers when I walk into the coffee shop, fingers pointing, cold stares. It was a very difficult decision. You can only fight so long, especially at this age. If any of my kids, or nieces and nephews for that matter, had shown any interest it would have been different. But it's not. All eight of them have gotten fancy degrees and moved out of the community. I reached out to every one of them to gauge their interest. It wasn't to happen.

Our family business kept the town alive for 85 years after the mines closed. We put bread on many a table, consoled families whose boys had gone off to war and not come back, allowed scores to go to college, and most of all kept the town safe and secure.

Not now. As I look at the vacant machines beginning to gather dust, I see the hundreds of faces who occupied those stations, hands working with a mind of their own, placing soles on boots bound for troops overseas.

What a family we created.

The keys in my hand rang out reminding me of my dark task. *The end justifies the means.* Isn't that what is always said about difficult controversial decisions?

I can still see my father's face as he handed me the ring. So proud, so confident, so hopeful. It was not to be, Dad.

Making the decision to close down our family business will haunt me for the remainder of my life. Saddling the next generation with crushing debt, a failing economy, and a dying industry is unconscionable. They'll thank me someday.

Facing the main factory door, I realize how heavy the keyring has become. It feels like an anchor hanging in my palm.

My fingers gently seek out the master key. This proud and glorious piece of well-worn metal slides smoothly into place, knowing its destiny. One half-turn of the wrist and we are closed forever.

Falling Ashes

My twitching hand made the cigarette's ashes rain to the ground.

My hands haven't trembled this much since I quit coke. Truth be told, I still miss the rush, the total oblivion, the orgasmic ability to just focus on *The Now.*

I can't think of that. I gotta concentrate.

Thanks be to Jesus; the kids would be living in some ratty foster home if I hadn't literally been pulled out of the alley. I still can't believe the church took us in for eight weeks till I got on my feet.

Lighting a smoke with the butt of the last, I let myself drift back to the first few days of sobriety. Initially, it was a bit disorienting to wake up in an unfamiliar bed, with clean sheets, the faint smell of wax and incense drifting through the air. Such a simple life. Those smells will forever take me back to the beginning of this path.

Gotta stay on the road, one day at a time, one

day at a time. Hit the meetings, push through with my sponsor, reach out to others. All good shit, all Christian shit really. Or perhaps I should say spiritual?

Holding the small crucifix in my free hand, I examine the grain in its wood, praying for the courage to fix this problem. I know I can. This is big. I'm not even sure I can wrap my head around what's going on. I've got to pull this off, it can change the rest of our lives. All our lives.

Like I'm entering a dream, I watch my hands straighten my apron, grab the cold doorknob, and pull, going back inside.

Cutting through the kitchen, I see my orders starting to build in the window, just like the noise. It always does when he's here. People are so willing to please, so greedy for attention.

That white noise, the buzz, it's a funny thing. One kid can't live with it and the other one can't live without it. He must sit in front of the radio to get his homework done while the other one must be locked in a monastery to get hers done.

I don't think anyone will ever know how important school has been to my children. It gave them a place to eat two meals a day, find kids that were kinda like them, and most importantly, it was a safe place to be while I exercised my demons.

Watching my nine-year-old do her homework last night, pencil firmly gripped in her long fingers. She was laser-focused. Something I never would have noticed before I went on the wagon. Watching her write a small paragraph with the same intensity I used when preparing my fix. She was on it. The light bounced off her auburn hair, creating a faint halo. She was miles away, oblivious to the music her brother was listening to while doing his homework.

I walked behind her trying to catch a glimpse of her paragraph and she slumped forward to cover it with her elbows. Ah yes, well played, my darling. I'll just wait till your asleep to take a peek.

After both kids were blissfully sleeping, I pulled her notebook out to read what she had been writing. One small paragraph, well-written in nine-year-old script, titled "Why I Love My Mommy When She's Not on Drugs."

I was crushed. Elated. Full of immense love and sorrow. How could this angel tell the harshest of truths? How did her small mind comprehend the last nine years? Her entire life?

I sat outside on the stoop for about 30 minutes, crying and laughing. It was only later, while running my hands through my wet hair, I realized it was softly raining. The type of rain you don't notice but somehow it washes away your sins. I thanked the Lord and fully accepted Him at that point. At that *very point.*

I must complete the task at hand for my little angels. Snapping back to reality, I grabbed the four plates ready to go, two in my hands, and two balancing on my forearms.

Here I go. I nudge the kitchen door open with my hip and enter the growing chaos.

Making my way past the obnoxious comments and the bodies of friendly drunks who come in for the never-ending cup of coffee, I find Table 32 and deliver their steak and eggs. Gotta love a place that serves all-day breakfast.

I get recognition from the thugs surrounding his table. These knuckle-dragging meatheads are on the job doing what they have to do in their own right to survive. They're here to protect this ass-hole who runs our neighborhood with an iron fist. Himself being a shit-stained product of everything wrong with our city.

Casually walking over with the water pitcher, I refill his glass and take his empty plate asking if everything was tasty.

"As tasty as it can be in this dump." Is what I expect to hear but don't.

"How long you been here, sweetheart? Do I know you?"

My mumbled answer makes him lean forward.

"I said, do I know you? 'Cause I'm pretty sure I do. Waz you hookin' a few streets over?" he asks.

My mind whirls, I pray my shaking voice and hands don't give me away.

I don't answer.

"That's it, yea, that's it, you were one of Johnny's girls over on 3RD who loved the dope."

"You all cleaned up now?

I slowly nod my head.

"That's good, that's good. Now I hate losin' a customer, but that's good, 'cause I asked around and know you got kids. Been saved by the church. I hate those bastards, always jumpin' into my business."

He reached into his jacket pocket and his immaculate hand pulled out a neatly rolled wad of cash. Peeling off a $50 bill, he hands it to me, grabbing my wrist as he does.

"Now I want you to take care of me when I'm here. Capisce?"

"Yes, Sir." Is all I can manage.

Wanting to throw up, I stuff the bill into my apron and retreat to the kitchen.

My God, he has no clue. None whatsoever. This fact drives in the last nail. My decision is made, there is no going back.

Grabbing my coat off the rack, I head outside to the phonebooth a block away.

This must be done.

Crushing out my cigarette, I watch my shaking fingers pick up the receiver, clicking the carrier to connect to the operator.

My hands are shaking so violently, I almost drop the phone, knowing this phone call will seal my fate, my children's fate. The weight of it all hits me like a brick.

"How may I connect you?"

"I need to talk to the Metro Detective Division please."

"Please hold the line, I'll connect you."

"Metro Police, how can I help you?"

"The man they been searching for is sitting right here in my coffee shop. At one of my tables."

My fingers search for and find my cigarettes hoping one will calm my nerves.

If he had only known. If he had only known my daughter was his. He was my first customer nine years ago setting me on a self-destructive path, ruining my world.

Until now.

If he had only known.

"You still there, Miss?"

"Yes, I'm still here. Is there still a $5,000 cash reward for the arrest and conviction of Alphonse Capone?"

The Impressionist

Man, I need to cut my nails. Every time I look at them, really look at them, I realize how quickly they grow. Unlike my bank account, right? What if, I mean, what if the length of your nails and hair reflected what was happening in your bank account? That'd be funny as hell!

"Yo, Lady, go out on a bender last night? Your nails are gone and what happened to your hair? You're bald as a cueball!"

"Yea, tied a wicked one on last night, and spent just about everything I had. No worries, its payday in a few days, I'll be brushing my hair in no time."

Now that would be funny as shit.

I started mentally drifting in and out, as my hand takes over. I love freaking people out when I switch hands, just kinda goes against the grain, doesn't it? I have Pops to thank for that talent. Spending summers with him and Gram on the beach, while Dad and Mom sucked up the exhaust of the city earning diddly. I guess they just got comfortable earning nada. Although now, somebody paying my insurance would sure as hell be nice. Damn, it's expensive!

Ole Pops, I sure do miss him. I can still feel his bear hug around my chest. Looking down, seeing his big claws laced together squeezing the air outta me. So vividly I picture his left thumb sticking out, the black nail, from when he and I were hammering boards on the porch the week before. Me distracting him with one of my many *What if* questions, and him smashing the shit right out of his left thumb. I learned a few new words that morning. Yea, I did.

But the left-handed talent? It started shortly after he yanked me out of the surf so fast I hardly had time to suck in any saltwater. Still a distinctly memorable tangy taste in my mouth right now. I can feel myself tumbling through the waves, right arm pinned behind me as the Narraganset sand came up and snapped my wrist. I can still hear it breaking, plain as day. Like a ball coming off Big Papi's bat at Fenway when he smashes one over the Big Green Monsta. Sound travels so clearly underwater. No crowd cheering, though, just the searing hot pain of my wrist crunching beneath me. Then the undertow grabbing hold of my body for the trip back out to into the Atlantic. Damn, the undertow was strong. Then the bearhug. Thank God for the bearhug.

The first thing he says after he made sure I wasn't dead? Classic Pops... "Now ya gonna hav'ta learn to draw with ya left hand, sweethaat, befor' school stats." Classic. Now look at me go, a double threat, made me famous up and down the coast.

His black and blue nail, such vivid colors. When was the last time he'd whacked himself so hard? It'd probably been years, or at least since Katrina, when he and his crew drove down to Louisiana and put themselves on the map with their building technique and speed. Now look where he is, one of the top Dawgs. Luck of the Irish, some of the jealous punks said at home.

"Dumb asses. If those retards had moved south when the money was ta be made, they'd be on tawp with me. Work ethic, Darlin, and timin', that's what it takes." He must have said it a thousand times if he'd said it once. And here I am having taken his old school advice.

Man, oh man, I miss that guy.

The muscles in my right hand always cramp first, reminding me to switch to southpaw. Flexing my right fingers, my left hand adapts to its new task. Red and blue, red and blue. I need to remember to order more of it for the shop. Seriously, if I told Ma how much I spent on those two colors per week, she'd shit her pants.

"My Gawd, we coulda put you through Juilliard. You freakin' kidding me?"

All day long, red and blue.

I do love getting into other colors, though. Quickly glancing at the Sunflower on the wall. A bit faded, but my best 13-year-old impression of Van Gogh. I loved tracing his swirls and gentle symmetric curves with my forefinger. How could such beauty come from such a tormented man? Not sure if I ever got into something so deeply as Vincent, even my final project at RISD. I'll have to check my computer for my files. I always love going through the research. So lost, yet unapparent to the folks who never take the time to do their homework. Maybe that's the way to do it, just look at the colors. Blue and red, blue then red.

My classmates thought I was crazy, all of them going on to other graphic arts shops along the East Coast.

"You have a degree from *Rhode Island School of Design,* girl, and you wanna do that? You're outta your mind," my bestie loved repeating on numerous occasions.

"Yea maybe, just got a feeling about this one, though, Ya know, just got a feeling."

Whirrrrrr, little dab, the white cotton soaking up the red.

"Never thought of that! Ha, how ironic. Funny watching blue blood turn red. Blue then red, red then blue. I'll have to write that one in my journal."

Wringing out my hand again, I pulled the skin-tight, making what was dimpled now smooth, a perfect place for Van Gogh to finish her work. As I trace the swollen, puffy area with my forefinger, it amazes me how these beautifully curved lines do look like Van Gogh's.

Squeezing my customer's shoulder with my left hand I recite my obligatory phrase. "All right, buddy, keep this clean, see your doctor if it gets gnarly, and we'll see you again next year when the Sox win the pennant. And don't forget to tell your buddies where you got it."

I run his card, hand over the receipt, then follow him out and lock the door. Quick twist of my tired hand turns the sign to "Closed".

Flipping the neon sign switch with my left thumb, I love hearing the sizzling and popping signifying to the world "Pops Tattoo Parlor", the most famous shop on the East Coast, is done for the day.

"Work ethic, Darlin', and timin', that's what it takes" rings through my mind.

The Signalman

"Bloody hell, my finger's sore."

Just a small flip of my fingernail every day reminds me of the man who I wanted to be, the man who had guided my life, steered me, taught me.

The light etching on the top of the gold case takes me back to the intermingled smell of burning peat and Grandad's pipe smoke. Strange how smells can trigger memories. How does your mind do that?

I cherish this time-piece. The one staring back at me, hands dancing along telling me its 11:32 PM, almost time for my shift. Beautiful, bold Roman numerals, ever reliable, swift and sweeping.

This watch drew me to the man. The countless tales of many an ocean's tempests, bar fights, and foreign maidens trying to change the course of this piece of gold's destiny. I've committed each and every tale to heart, burying them deep in my memory. "Auch Bay, 30 years in Her Majesty's service, if t'was a day!" signaled the end of every tale.

Damn, I better hurry. Jack's probably still got a stack of Marconigram messages to send to the Cape Race Station from those needy Yanks. Enjoyable blokes for the most part, not as entitled as our aristocrats, at least the ones I met in Southampton.

Snapping the lid shut with my thumb, always loving the metallic click, I once again stow my watch. My memory conjures up the feel of Grandad's rough palm as he pressed his beloved friend into my hand, gifting me its destiny, our destiny, his palm so worn by the caresses of many a working line. Not a day goes by I don't think of him.

I've tried to remember if I have ever been as infatuated with anything as I am with my latest mistress. I love the feel of her new brass doorknobs, not yet worn by the test of time. The smooth woodwork of her railings, gentle English curves, made for the seeking hand in need of support during rough seas. Not sticky yet from the constant harassment of the cool salt air. This ship was done right, yes she was. And I was honored to be among her first.

I could feel "it" before I could see "it". Whatever "it" is makes the hair on the back of one's neck stand up, just before "it" happens. In those split seconds my mind envisioned the feeling as a thick, foreboding early morning London fog creeping through a dark, damp alley.

Then a physical shudder. Is that real or is my

mind working in concert with my heightened emotional state? Then I saw the first clue and an invisible fist violently punched my stomach.

The Captain positioned himself right behind Jack with his feet firmly planted on the discarded sent messages, now littering the floor. People's written thoughts and well-wishes, scattered on the highly polished planks, stubbornly sticking like fall leaves after a rain. Very odd.

I could see the Captain's snow-white beard moving in concert with the unspoken words as his stubby wide hand wrote out the first of many messages Jack and I would hammer out on this historic evening. He nimbly tore it from his message tablet, folded it in half, signaling we were not to read it yet and pressed it into Jack's waiting palm.

"Lads, I pray to the Lord you won't have to send this. DO NOT, I repeat, DO NOT, read it until I return."

Turning to leave for the bridge, that gentleman's fingers sternly grabbed me by the crux of the elbow, digging into the nerve, making my hand go numb.

"Son, we have work to do." He released me from his grip and spun toward the bridge. "God save us," trailing from his lips like steaming smoke from the lead stack.

Time played its trick on me again by slowing to a virtual standstill. What a fickle master Time can be. Cloaking its constant drumbeats behind the veil of the lightning fast or the glacial crawl. Never bartered nor won back with the roll of the dice. Quarter always asked, never given…

Now alone in the room, as Jack had stepped out for a smoke, Grandad's watch witnessed the passage of 20 minutes since the Captain departed. No sooner had my finger snapped the lid back shut did he burst into our message room. His coal-black eyes boring into me, "Send it! I have confirmation. Send it! And keep sending it, till someone is steaming towards us!"

"Aye, Aye Sir!" Was all I could muster. My fingers gently unfolded the creased paper, stopping my heart.

I prayed my finger would be touched by God, both accurate and fast. A momentary flashback to my first piano teacher's fingers gliding across the keyboard, slim, unadorned, yet carrying an unseen strength. Make mine more like hers, Lord.

I hadn't noticed Jack coming back into the room as I had become one with the machine. My message hand having taken on a life of its own, hammering out a whole different language, so foreign to the untrained, but a symphonic electronic conversation to those of us in the know. Milliseconds later Jack comprehended what I was tapping out.

"Blimey! What in God's name are you tapping that out for!" Jack yelled in a voice so rich with desperation it was palpable.

— ·— · — — ·— — ·· — ·· — ·— — — ·· — ·—·
C   Q   D   TI T A   NI C

···— ·— — — — ····— ····— — · ····· — — — — — ··— —
— ····— · — —
4   1   4 4N 5   0   2   4 W

— ·— · — — · — — ·· — ·— · — — · — — ·· — ·—
· — — ·— — ··
C   Q   D   C   Q   D

ALL STATIONS DISTRESS   ALL STATIONS DISTRESS

None of my Grandad's tales ever involved anything like this. This couldn't be happening.

Jack's hands became vice grips on my shoulders. "What are you doing, Harry?!"

"We've hit an iceberg Jack, we've hit an iceberg!"

— ·— · — — ·— — ·· — ·· — ·— — — ·· — ·—·
C   Q   D   TI T A   NI C

···— ·— — — — ····— ····— — · ····· — — — — — ··— —
— ····— · — —
4   1   4 4N 5   0   2   4 W

— ·— · — — · — — ·· — ·— · — — · — — ·· — ·—
· — — ·— — ··
C   Q   D   C   Q   D

ALL STATIONS DISTRESS   ALL STATIONS DISTRESS

Monday Morning

I love the feel of the early morning ripping through my hair. Sometimes it almost peels the skin right off my face. Only a thin piece of leather between my calloused palm and the rolled metal as I hang there clutching like a monkey on a branch.

Need to make a slight adjustment, particularly going this speed, and all's good.

Fingers locked back in again, foot firmly planted on the step, other one swinging in the air, as if I were sitting with Grandma on the side of the porch, shucking corn. Damn those husks used to tear my little fingers up.

It might have been the only time Grandma and I got to spend alone. She'd give me a head nod while passing through the kitchen, and off we'd go. Her hands gently holding the bushel basket with all the silky corn hair poppin' out, waiting for its freedom. It was all fun till it got stuck to your bibs. Then you'd have to pick it off one strand at a time.

Grandma would pat the side of the porch swing

and invite me up to commence the job.

And oh, the stories she would tell about her victory garden during WWII. Corn, squash, green beans, the whole deal. It was tough feeding 13 kids during the 40s.

She'd eventually plop a piece of corn in the waterless pot and lifting her hand pointing to the family plot where three brothers now resided courtesy of the Nazis, and one from the ghastly trip up Mount Iwo Jima. All came home to rest. She'd never fail to mention her twin sister, either, killed while shuttling a B52 cross country to its embarkation point. "Debbie had more flight time than most of them boys. That's for certain. Hmmm Hm, that's for certain. Father Time was in a bloody mood back then," she'd lament, not missing a husk nor hair with her nimble fingers.

Such tragedy made such a beautiful stone garden. Grandma's the newest flower. I feel her hand upon my shoulder when times are challenging.

This morning's a bit chilly, hard to believe it's late August already. Kids going back to school next week.

I'd always see the results, too. My hands ache from it, my arms burn at the end of the day as a result of it. Kids having shot up by leaps and bounds, outgrowing clothes, summer sneakers, crayons, notebooks, the whole list goes on. The kids always love getting the new school supply list.

Some of those things I never pass up though. Slightly used, no problem. Pastor Phil is in such a need of children's items after his summer camps. The "Hand of Jesus" Camps my kids call them because my wife would beller out "You better get in the car on time or you're going to feel the Hand o' Jesus Himself on your backside!"

A smile creeps across my face as I conjure up the kids running through the trailer at night, barking dogs in hot pursuit as they mimic her. "Hand o' Jesus... Hand o' Jesus." My wife too slow to catch any of the scurrying rascals, and, like all parents, secretly enjoying the moment, knowing soon there will be other, more life-altering times, when she'll be using that phrase.

"Oh man, look at that. Almost a full box of books and two pencil cases full of stuff."

"Thank you very much, always a pleasure doing business with you!" I murmur.

I can always count on the Walmsleys this time of year. Good Irish Catholics with money to spare. Who wouldn't with such a thriving family business? They've been taking care of the dead in this community since the early 1800s. Mr. Walmsley certainly looks the part. Tall, shrunken face, arms down to his knees, and boney, boney hands. Veins always popping out of the top. Used to creep me out when he shook my hand knowing he had touched all the dead folks I had known.

Unfortunately, I'm over that now, having lived through enough tragedy in this small town to really appreciate what he does. No doubt he's good, offering comfort and peace of mind.

Shirt's starting to stick to my back. Now there's the August sun and good old South Carolina humidity.

Jump down, grab, lift with the knees, shuffle, shuffle, fling, grab the bar, step up, feel the air.

Same old Monday routine. There's always something freeing about helping people with their problems. Just amazing to see how families make their decisions. Particularly the ones I know or went to high school with.

Time and time again, sitting in Deano's Tap Room, caressing a nice dewy bottle of beer, grubby fingertip tracing the drops racing to the bar top, I want to approach some of the folks I know and ask them how they could do that? Don't they know our sweet earth is a gift and not being good stewards will ultimately catch up to our children? Our children's children? It's already apparent in some Third World countries.

Now those foreign folks are facing some major issues, particularly when it comes to air and water pollution. Not to mention soil conservation. Damn, take a look around people!

Such waste.

Air brakes interrupt my constant internal monolog.

Jump down, grab, lift with the knees, shuffle, shuffle, fling, grab the bar, step up, feel the air.

Now, where was I? Yes, the environment, my passion. As a proud father of five, I can say my kids will be Champions of Mother Earth. We raised 'em that way. Grandma taught me, I'm teaching them.

Best to take a route of action with kids. No one ever really seems to take me seriously.

Suddenly I hear my partner's voice, "Need some help over here."

Pulling my gloves on a bit tighter, fingertips ripping out, nails starting to protrude. I round the truck to see a weary old couch, no doubt holding crumbs, dog hair, and about $3.23 in coins, waiting on me.

My partner's exasperated look telling it all. "Can you believe these people? Such a waste."

"Yea Buddy," is all I can muster.

My aching hands grab the arm of the old veteran couch and heave. This fella will now grace our blessed earth with its presence, keeping the memories of so many movies, Super Bowls, and nightly news all to itself.

Like we all will.

But what do I know?

I hang my ass off the side of a garbage truck every day.

Jump down, grab, lift with the knees, shuffle, shuffle, fling, grab the bar, step up, feel the air.

He's Got a Cannon

Man, my stomach's rolling again. It happens every time I come down to this God-forsaken island. I need to learn not to drink the first cerveza at the airport bar. Looking at my fingers tightly curled around a second beer, I clearly haven't learned not to. They just taste so damn refreshing.

I do love watching the sweat gather at the top, then trickle down past my thumb and forefinger, leaving a clear trail on the bottle in its wake. Quickly gaining speed through the path of least resistance, the sweat gently eases its way into my palm. Yea, my fingers always taste like a hint of lime from the bartender squeezing a wedge of it into the anticipating ale.

Tilting the bottle back and forth I can see Ms Lime Wedge dancing to the bottle top trying to escape her new home. Nope, senorita, you're not getting outta there, you'll rest comfortably at the bottom when I drain the last drop.

Chasing the last chunk of fish around the ceviche plate, I have a few minutes for a smoke, find my seat, and settle in to see if I've made another trip for nothing.

Unfailingly, I go through my routine which takes me back to my maiden voyage to Yankee Stadium.

Dad's slight hand squeezing my shoulder as we came out of the upper deck to gaze upon the emerald green field for the first time. Still gives me goosebumps, even in this sweltering 102°.

My fingers absently peel the bottle label off as I take my inevitable trip down memory lane. With my father being a career bookkeeper at the local bank, I never dreamed I'd be in the "Cathedral" staring down as the Red Sox took the field for one of the most heated rivalries in the world. That day was an epic duel as The Babe had just been traded to N.Y.! Our family didn't have a ton of money, especially for the 12th kid, but it was my turn to go, so Pops kept his promise, much to the disappointment of my six brothers.

While gathering up my satchel to find my seat, my mind's eye sees Dad's nimble fingers dancing over the scoresheet explaining all of the mystical boxes, what they meant, when to fill them in, when not to. It was one of the most exhilarating, yet thoroughly confusing times I can remember. A numbers man instilling the spirit of America's pastime in his son.

Ah yes, Pops said it was all in the process, the routine if you were going to become an expert scorekeeper. He'd be delighted to know I'd handed down his method to his three grandsons.

At the end of the day I still love this sport. Tonight's heat and humidity are testing that resolve as my fingers pull the soaking shirt collar from my neck. Looking at my fedora, the growing salted sweat stain stands witness to how the sun can bake you to the core sitting here in the scorching heat trying to discover the next prodigy.

My fingers unfurl tonight's program checking for my assignments. I have a few guys to watch; two pitchers, a right fielder, and, of course, the shortstop. Everyone's after him. I haven't talked to him yet, but I know the Yankees and the Dodgers have. It's tough pulling Latino kids to a place like the upper Midwest, far away from the major Hispanic populations. They'll take less money to get closer to relatives who "habla." I've heard the Dominicans aren't quite like that but looks like I'll find out in a few days in Santo Domingo.

All about the routine… sharpen the pencil, grab a bag of peanuts, get out my binoculars and settle in. Hoisting my spyglass, I scan the boys taking the field. Looks like two of my guys are starting; one at short and the other on the mound.

The public announcer confirms the right fielder isn't in the lineup. Crap. Looks like the newspaper was right, said his esposa caught him in bed with another senorita. She smashed two of his fingers with an iron. Looking at my own fingers, I couldn't imagine how that felt. Especially for a baseball player.

I put his mangled fingers out of my mind and started focusing on my pitcher's mechanics as he began his routine. I like it. Fingers nimbly maneuver the ball as he inspects it, flipping his glove to the catcher, his other fingers now finding the threads. Arms come up slowly in connection with his legs. The release is smooth, so smooth. My mental abacus makes the calculations on his potential and I keep him on the "A" list.

Here we go… Leadoff batter pops up on the second pitch, high and inside, good placement. Shortstop got right underneath it, routine play. The second batter lays down a nice bunt and the ball trickles toward third base, having a conversation with each piece of grass it touches. Beautiful job. The pitcher scoops it up firing to first about a half stride too late.

While I'm jotting down notes on this pitcher's delivery, the runner advances to second base on a low outside curveball which squirts past the catcher. Man, "catch" has been in the league forever. He needs to move on so some young stud with good defensive skills can test his luck.

The crack of the wooden bat, one of my all-time favorite sounds, brings my head out of my notebook. I stand with the rest of the crowd. This one has a chance. It's a high line drive curving toward the corner fence. Ah, its gonna be short…

What I see next is a life changing moment. A piece of history actually. My hands instinctively clutch the stadium railing, holding it so tightly my knuckles turn absolutely white, pencil innocently tumbling to the ground, rolling into the aisle.

The tall lanky kid in right field, who hadn't made the least bit of an impression on me during pregame warm up, perfectly reads the ball. Playing the corner angles instinctively, like he'd been there his whole life, gracefully maneuvering towards his prey.

He's on the ricocheting ball in a second, footwork so quick and expertly placed, I know no coach had ever taught him that. He just did it. I bet if you asked him how he knew where to place his feet, no way he could tell you. This kid was beyond athletic, he was a natural.

Shielding my eyes from the setting sun, I see the second base runner streaking around for third. The cutoff man's screaming in Spanish for the ball, arms outstretched and waving.

A chill ran down my spine as the right fielder instantaneously made his decision, seamlessly transitioned the ball to his throwing hand, planted, and fired it towards the infield. My heart sank as I realize he'd overshot the cutoff man. Rookie mistake. The crowd moaned but without losing a breath instantly erupted in unison realizing he's throwing for the runner. He's throwing to the plate!

The runner hears the crowd and takes an outside line for home.

The ball rockets over the cutoff man's glove and carries to three inches above the dirt into the catcher's outstretched mitt, for a classic, dust-filled collision at the plate. As the dirt cloud settles, the catcher's hand immerges, held high, clutching the ball. The crowd goes insane, absolutely wild, not knowing the historic significance of the moment.

I quickly look out to rightfield and see the lanky young man turning his back to the play adjusting his cap assuming his position. Back to work. Humble can go a long way in this sport.

Man, I like this kid. He's a keeper.

Searching through the program I locate the rightfielder's name. I open my notebook and watch my hand write four simple words next to his name, changing the baseball world forever.

#18 Roberto Clemente. **He's got a Cannon**

God's Own Hands

It was the Lord's own hands that delivered the colt. My God, no doubt, because it sure as hell wasn't mine. Staring down at my bloody arms, wrists, and fingers, thoughts begin ricocheting off the walls of my brain. It's always amazing how my hands can become so clean after an ordeal like the birth of some creature. It takes a bit of extra scrubbing to wash off the blood, mucus, and mare's membrane, but they're soon spotless again.

The first delivery honestly made me sick to the point of the dry heaves, tasting the barf coming up. Not anymore, after thousands of little ones gracing our world in my presence, it's just the beautiful circle of life.

Always funny how the birthing conversation with my buddies seems to come up around beers or dinner time. It escalates quickly when our wives are with us. "Oh, yea? I had to get the strap, hook it to my trailer hitch and pull that calf out. Turns out there were four of them in there! Hey Honey, pass over more chicken, would ya?" Everyone roars with laughter, looks of feigned disgust from the ladies and the conversation changes to some other subject which also ends up in the mud.

What a crowd: chiseled, weathered, and a bit beaten. Like theirs, you can see the wrinkles of time gathering on my hands. Very distinct lines developing, each well-deserved, each having a story of its own. Some serious and some to the point of gut-splitting laughter. So, so many, half of which I've forgotten over the years.

Dinnertime conversations always take me back to when I was a sprout listening to my father and his friends. Yup, apple hasn't fallen far from the tree. My hands are a mirror image of his. I can see his fingers in mine. Strangest thing, really, it's the strangest thing. I remember one night, in his later years, we were waiting for a few of our sows to deliver, sitting beside each other, clutching onto the homemade farrowing crate, when I announced I wanted to go to the state agricultural college to become a large animal vet.

"Son, let me give you a few good reasons to think about bein' a farm vet."

What ensued were the details, history really, of his life working the land, fixing machinery, raising children, animals and even adults. He used his scarred hands and fingers as a road map, each a harsh lesson of country life.

No kidding, by the time he was done it was like a course in agricultural and world history over the last 72 years. I had always noticed his scars, but now, like his, mine told a similar tale.

He started with the large scar right up his left palm. If you didn't pay attention, you'd think it was just one lifeline a palm reader at the county fair would focus on, telling of your impending fame and fortune.

But this one, this one was a doozy, and amazingly enough, very special to him. See, he'd served as a tanker in General Patton's 3rd Corps during WWII, fighting across Europe, liberating the continent from the Nazi horde. As he told the story, he'd flex his hand slightly to see the scar move, crinkle, get lost in his palm, then reappear again.

"I earned this scar kicking Nazi ass in a fierce battle in a small French town. We had just taken out two panzers when I saw a horse flailing in the mud trying to free itself. See, son, he was joined with another gelding who had been killed in the fight and there was no way that poor animal was goin' anywhere unless somebody helped him. So, I dismounted 'AmySue' (the M42 Sherman tank he called home, named after their Lieutenant's fiancé) to assist the beast. I laid my hand on the animal and his worn muscles shivered under my palm. My God, he was a sweating mess. So much good livestock died in the war. I grabbed his rigging with my left hand, pulled out my K Bar knife, and just as I began slicing through the leather, I hear the man himself, no shit, General Patton yell, 'Son! What the Hell are you doing!'"

My knife went right through the leather and straight up my left palm.

At that point in the tale I instinctively ran my finger across his palm, feeling that small piece of history.

He gently traced the jagged line from beginning to ragged end. As his story went, General Patton dismounted, climbed through the mud and gore to help him liberate the struggling horse. "Damn good job, son. Now let's go kick some German ass! What'do ya say?" How many others can tell a war story like that?

My hands always, no matter what the physical dimensions, looked small compared to my father's. Even at one of the last church services we attended together I watched him hold the prayer book, his hands still outwardly possessed the strength of a man who had spent his life attempting to bend the earth to his will. Mother Nature acquiesced on occasion but in most instances, certainly did not. The preacher was discussing the Lord being the Alpha and the Omega and how many of those in his congregation witnessed that cycle many times over the course of their lives. The Beginning and the End.

Between us, how many times had he and I seen the full cycle? Birthing a creature only to guide it through an existence with the sole purpose of eventually taking it to market, providing sustenance to those close to me and many I would never meet.

Another of his favorite scars was in the center of his left thumb which had a matching scar on the upper portion of the thumb on the opposite side, right under the cuticle.

Each summer after he and his brothers brought the hay in, they'd take a week-long fishing trip to Canada. Now with me and my cousins having boys, the trip had grown exponentially as did the chaos. This scar was from the last of the trips when my son, at the tender age of eight, began his cast and inadvertently caught Dad's thumb with one of those big lake trout treble hooks. Sucker went right through his thumb. I had to cut the barb off and pull it the rest of the way out. Thank goodness the beer had been flowing up till that point. Great family story.

If I had one thing to do again with my dad, it would be to capture every one of his stories through his road map of scars. As a matter of fact, if I could write worth a damn, I'd write a book based solely on the stories told through the scars on my family's hands. I'd love to have that on my shelf.

"What's that, Honey? Time to leave for the fair? Be right there, just need to jot a few things down."

First Encounter

Another rock in my glove? Seriously?

How many times do I need to put 100-mile-an-hour tape over that rip? Those damn finite rocks just grate the skin right off the bone. Amazing how small they are. Somewhere between a pebble and sand. It's like the good Lord takes a boulder and gently rolls it between His thumb and forefinger until it comes down to this teeny, tiny piece of stone just meant to slip into the top of my glove, over my palm, down to the fingertip and rest there, working the skin, or one of my favorites, getting under my fingernail. Then again, why go in the top of my glove when that little tear is the best shortcut to my now-calloused fingertips?

It's a piece of earth you can't crush, like Peter, the Lord's cornerstone. Not a craggy boulder as I envision him, but a finite, independent rock, not to be denied, fitting on your fingertip. My bet as to its geological phase? Sand. Most definitely sand.

Well, maybe I'll patch the hole by turning my glove inside out and taping it. That might work. Hadn't thought of that.

Hours and hours of boredom out here shattered by minutes of terror. Isn't that what they say?

The sky is so beautiful here in the mountains, stars for miles, no light pollution to cut into the serenity. Just like Montana.

Mom blew my mind yesterday when she reminded me the boiling sun I was roasting under was actually the same sunshine lighting up the moon over our ranch. She turned the computer camera around so I could see it. What an experience. Almost broke down, but didn't, as she'd be crushed.

Mom was coasting on her favorite piece of furniture, our porch's squeaky glider, while her hands methodically created rural art, its destiny only existing in her mind at this point. Those weathered hands translating a mental image into something someone would love to wear.

Some of the native women here would look beautiful in one of her scarves. Their light ebony or grey eyes would pop right out of their faces with the colors Mom would select for them. She could sell a million scarves in this land of burkas. Wouldn't that be ironic? I can see Shark Tank now… "Soldier's mom makes a million bucks selling scarves to the enemy." Go figure...

Even though I have never desired to knit, I always marveled at her fingers working the needles. Tips gliding over the silky yarn so quickly it was hard to keep up. All the time she'd carry on a conversation with us, scolding us, mentoring us, counting purls and knits in her head.

We hardly noticed as we rolled across the deck in one of our never-ending wrestling matches. Wrestling is still fun now but took a bit of a turn when baby brother's testosterone kicked in. Dad's bellowing voice still echoes in my mind "Let your sister up, you're getting too big for that." My twin brother would ease up, let me squirm loose, and I'd deliver the coup de grâce, the winning blow, a snappy shot to the crotch. Dad winced, as if I'd given him the parting blow, like all men do when a comrade suffers this fate, and start to chuckle, his hands laced on his growing belly. All about the "W". Not too many sisters can say they bested the 198 lb. Montana State Wrestling Champion at his own game. I did, and have the witnesses to prove it!

What the hell is that? The little rock in my glove now a distant memory as my forefinger slips the safety off my weapon.

"Renegade 32, this OP 3, Over. Movement in sector Alpha, Over."

"Roger, OP 3, we picked it up on the ground sensors."

What the hell is that? Got it. The green glow of my night vision scope making out the form crawling toward me in the bush. Red dot anticipating its next move. Unfortunately, I may know mine.

"Renegade 32, this OP 3, Over. It's a dog."

"Roger out, OP 3."

Dogs, dogs, dogs. They're all over the place. How can they even survive when half the people around here look like they haven't eaten in weeks? With all the activity lately, this K9's lucky I didn't pop him.

Damn, little fella is making his way up here. I know we aren't supposed to feed 'em or even touch 'em cause of the diseases.

Crap, it's a puppy. I think he may have smelled my MRE. Good old spaghetti with meat sauce would have Wolfgang Puck himself walking across a free-fire zone. That shit's tasty.

He's onto me. Ohhh be careful! A claymore is right about where you're standing.

Cool, he saw it. Now around the two trip flares. Past one, Good boy, now slide to your left, that's two. Ok, last thing is my partner 50 feet away in that pit he calls a foxhole. He loves to light up animals, not sure why. If he'd grown up hunting, instead of sitting his fat ass on the couch in whatever piece of crap town he's from, he would have appreciated how delicate the balance of life is. K, knucklehead must be sleeping, cause he missed him.

"Hey, don't stop and sniff, ya big dummy, you're almost here." If this little fella makes it, I'm going to give him my Blackfoot name, "Two Guns." I was named after one of our famous chiefs from many years ago. Plus, at this very snippet in time, he has at least two guns trained on him.

"Come on, Two Guns, you can do this." My gloved hand now pinching the top of my dinner, wrist waving it in the air. That's gotta be letting some smell out, right?

He caught it, he caught it.

"Come on in here, Two Guns." Man, he's a keeper. Must have figured out the game, 'cause he's plump, yea buddy, he's roly-poly.

I pull my gloves off to start stroking his head. Look at him eat! I'll get some heat for this, but who cares, Two Gun's a keeper. And when I tell my Platoon Sergeant the Legend of the Blackfeet and how Chief Two Guns lead many raids making our people who they are today, there's no way he won't let me keep him in the FireBase.

Maybe, maybe he'll let me take him back to Camp Phoenix. Man, that'd be cool, my personal fuzzball. I know a guy over in 2nd Battalion who actually put in a request to Headquarters and got to take his dog home to treat his PTSD. Got plenty of that going around. Everyone should get a freakin' dog.

My fingertips kneading his skin, his fur is a little frumpy, but so soft. I can feel his ribs on both sides, too. That fuzz was hiding his skeleton.

Holding his jaw in my palm, I ask "All done, Buddy? Hey, your breath smells like meat sauce, little turd, you ate it all." There it is, the puppy breath! Two Guns grew up in the 'Stan and still has the same puppy breath like our blue healers at home. How can that be? I love that smell.

"Now settle in TG, we have about an hour left to go before we rotate. Then, I sneak your scrawny ass past First Sergeant and introduce you to the fellas. They're gonna Looooovvve you!"

"OP3, SITREP, Over."

"Renegade 6, this is OP3, nothing significant to report."

"Roger Out."

They're gonna love you. Yes sir, they will.

All righty, let's get down to business.

Damn that tear, I think it's gotten bigger.

Not Bad

Just think, all my friends right now are rolling into school.

It's always difficult getting the mud off the face of my watch. No matter how hard or gentle my grubby fingers rub, my watch-face is still scratched and filthy. Breathing on the glass and fogging it up helps clean it somewhat, but after 18 months of beating up this timepiece it's showing wear. I'm mesmerized as my finger does its ritual laps around the face. Realizing a bit of moisture is now under the glass, it saddens me to think it's on borrowed time. See what I did there? Not long now before I'll need to strip one off the wrist of a rotting corpse.

1430. Let's see, take six hours from that, making it 0830 in Ohio. My buddies are just leaving homeroom. What the hell was I thinking? Just had to follow in my brother's footsteps.

My fingertips brushed over prickly morning stubble, not soft like it would be in a few days. I thank my ancestors for the dark shadow making me look five years older, or should I thank them?

I still find it hard to believe my recruiter bought off on me being 18. I guess the push across Europe was making Uncle Sam desperate to get as many boys in boots as possible. We need 'em, that's for certain.

Well here I am, seeing Europe for the first time. "Dear Mom, France is beautiful this time of year!" Waving my arm across the gorgeous countryside our general selected for the next battleground.

Funny though, when I told my buddies I actually enlisted, they slapped me on the back, pumped my hand, and gave me bearhugs leading to our never-ending wrestling matches. Everyone was so proud, I still haven't written to tell them what job I actually ended up with. That'll be for another time. A time I can properly tell the story.

1440. Everyone's leaving homeroom for their first class.

In my mind's eye, I can still see my father's hands neatly folded on the dinner table, like stone, not flinching, realizing this was something I had to do. Much like he did, the desire to become a U.S. citizen by standing up for justice during the First Great War.

Months before, I witnessed my brother break the news, giving me a bit of insight into what the moment would be like. My announcement was received differently. Pops said very little. Mother's hands, in typical Italian tradition, talking for her.

Bursts of pride and fear mingling as she clutched her rosary with a shaking right hand, lace handkerchief in the left, berating me in Italian and broken English. At the end of her tirade she made me promise, then swear, I wouldn't enlist for the infantry. One son in the infantry broke her heart. Two would be her death. I didn't have the courage to tell her I already had.

During Basic Training God showed His sense of humor. He reached right down, took his big finger, and poked me square in the eye. He made me uphold the oath I had sworn to my mom. With that poke in the eye he ensured I couldn't hit a target from five feet away. Couldn't hit water if I was swimming in it. I can still hear my drill sergeant's voice booming every time we marched down range to check our practice targets. "Sweet God Almighty, Meatball! How in the hell can you miss a paper target from 25 feet? The German's ain't gonna be standing still flapping in the breeze, son! You better get right with whatever God you pray to!"

Clink, clink, clink, my own filthy fingernail tapping on my watch face brings me back to reality. It was time to get started.

Shuffling to the tent, I was still amazed at how much mud a bunch of humans could make in a short time. We hadn't even bivouacked for two days, just enough to get set up, and this place was a huge, sloppy mess.

June rains didn't help. My father, being a self-professed premier winemaker, would love these rolling French hills. "Perfetto per il Vino!" Poppa was classic. He'd hold up his latest creation, announce it followed the oldest family recipe from the hills of Sicily, kiss the bottle, then thrust his cradling hands in the air. "Ohhh, youa gonna lika thisa one!" The family would cheer, and the cork would unleash the secrets of our ancestors!

Family recipes are what kept me in the Army. In Basic Training, on platoon competition day, my drill sergeant was trying to figure out where to hide me during the platoon marksmanship competition. "Hey Meatball, you ain't shootin today," he booms. "Get down to the mess hall and help Cookie with chow."

"YES, DRILL SERGEANT!" and off I ran.

I can still see my dirty hand push open the mess hall door exposing my true calling. Strange how destiny can reach up and smack you right across the face. I think Cookie saw fate's handprint on my cheek as soon as I reported to him.

"You *Eye-Talion*, Son?"

"YES, COOKIE, SIR!"

"Then get your garlic-smellin' ass over to that bowl and start makin' the meatballs. The boys is gettin' pasta today."

The rest goes down into the annals of family history. I was quickly shipped off to Ft. Lee, Virginia, to the Army's culinary arts training school. Yes, my destiny was to become a United States

Army "Spoon". Perhaps one of the most loved positions in the Military.

The thing they didn't teach you in culinary training was the battlefield stuff. Every meal we made in school was for the General.

Where the hell was I supposed to get saffron and oregano in this God-forsaken French mudhole? Plus, three days ago my chow wagon had taken the best artillery round the Krauts could offer, leaving me with very little to work with.

My mind began to inventory what was left. Chow time was in less than an hour and my Dawg Faces are always starving before an impending battle.

Very surreal knowing you could be feeding a man his last meal.

- Large boiling pot
- Small boiling pot
- Three frying pans
- Salt, pepper, garlic
- Local scallions I found in the field
- Lard
- Butter
- Side of Beef
- Shit ton of local potatoes and carrots

My mind and hands became one. The other two "Spoons" on duty stepped aside becoming my sous chefs, knowing I was in the zone, prepping only the little things and handing me ingredients when asked.

When I was a kid I witnessed my nonna and Ma in this moment. They'd hustle around the stove, hardly measuring anything, finishing each other's sentences. Nonna making small corrections, orchestrating a gastronomic masterpiece for 14 people packed around a loud family table.

Another day's chow complete! I had no bottle of homemade vino to hold up, but I was certain all would leave the chow hall stuffed to the gills, ready to deal death and destruction upon the Germanic Hordes.

The ruckus in an Army chow hall is legendary. However, on this day a lull descended on the boys. Hardly a word was spoken. It was extremely unsettling, just murmurs. A shiver ran down my spine as I heard what all spoons dread. The Command Sergeants Major gravelly voice...

"Cookie! Get your Goat Stinkin' Ass out here right now! On the Double!"

"YES, SERGEANTS MAJOR!!" My God. Was I back in Basic Training? Can't hit a target, can't cook a meal?

"Cookie! My warriors have said nothing during chow! You are entirely to blame for this! They are too busy stuffing their war-loving, Nazi-killing, pie-holes with whatever you call this miserable piece of filth taking up the precious space on my sacred mess kit."

My arms were locked so tightly behind my back I thought I was going to pass out. My face started to twitch, brow and hands sweating profusely.

"What do you claim to call this miserable assault on my palate, Cookie!?"

"SERGEANTS MAJOR, THAT'S CALLED A FRENCH FRY, SERGEANTS MAJOR!"

"As God is my witness, Cookie, this is the best damned concoction I have eaten in years! You will stuff my soldiers with this heavenly deeelight until their sides burst!"

"Do you understand me, Cookie?!"

"YES, SERGEANTS MAJOR!"

Perfecto!

Make it Happen Again

My arms are going to break off.

No way to hold my hands above my head too much longer.

I know I saw it here first and the smell and black color on the ground are what tells me I am right.

The air is getting too cold for me to stand here. My fingertips and feet are starting to tingle. When the yellow ball sits on the animal for a long time, it makes the animal's cover come off. Then it is so much easier to pull the meat from the bones and chew. Much easier. Much better.

I know she liked it, too. I could tell by her face she liked me bringing it to her.

Of all the ones left, she is the one I want. Now just to catch her.

Never have I seen one so fast. I think it is something from her side of the water.

The old one said their food is running out. She holds up her old hand and with crooked fingers points up and says, "This many times and times again is when they came here last."

Me and the rest do not know how long ago it was, but she tells us it was a bad time for all. Very cold.

She tells of the oldest one left. He has only one foot. He lost the other one when it turned black and fell off from the cold. Her toothless smile always appears as she waddles around with one leg bent, thumping her chest like he does. All of the young ones laugh.

I see many pictures like this girl on the walls in the place where we sleep. Running fast with many like her. Long hair back behind them, arms in the sky, hands upward stretched to the yellow ball in the sky.

Must find a way to bring her closer.

Must make it work again. For her.

I jump and grab the stick above me and start to swing on it in the air. Pulling it against the other one right below it. This must be how it was working.

"*Ahhh, ughhh*" goes the air from my mouth after the sticks break and I fall to the dirt. The ground is now soft, with tree skin and brown coverings.

I heard other sticks cracking as I walk on them.

Lying on the soft dirt, looking up, I see something bounce off the others, making it look again like before. The coverings have almost all fallen like they do before the cold comes and the water turns hard.

The yellow ball brings a tingling feeling on my skin. I cover my eyes from it to see the animals who are trying to move away. I put my hand in front of me and move my knobby fingers back and forth, separating them.

It comes in and goes out. It comes in and goes out, making my eyes hurt as it peeks through. The faster I move my fingers, the quicker this happens and each time the feeling comes in. Just a little.

This is also the tingling coming from me when I trap her to the ground and move back and forth with her, making the feeling.

I slowly get to my hands and knees still clutching the broken stick I was hanging on.

With the other, I sweep these tree coverings toward me to make them into a small pile.

Now to make the feeling and see the warmness bounce off the others.

Another small stick is lying nearby, my fingers close around it.

The rubbing with her is what made the warm feeling for me and the dancing of the tree is what made the warmness move on my hand and face.

Placing one stick upon the other I make them dance together. Nothing.

Faster, like in the end with her.

I see my hands move faster. Nothing.

Faster. Faster. My wind runs out.

I look down and the stick is now in the mud.

I pick one stick up and place it on the hard rock.

Faster, faster, faster. A small white snake appears from the stick.

I stop and watch as the snake disappears with the wind.

My arms now feel pain. But faster they must go.

Again, faster, the snake comes back. The stick skin comes loose and falls to the tree coverings, and the snake gets bigger.

My hand feels it.

There it is! There it is!

The white snake grows and covers me. Floats around me as a tiny tongue reaches to the other coverings and grows.

This tongue is almost the color of the inside blood of animals.

I see my hands go faster again making the sticks dance.

The tongues are growing, eating the tree covering. The warmness from above is now in this small pile of sticks and coverings.

It is here now!

I have found how to make this come to us. The fast sticks are making the white snake appear!

The tongues now dance in the wind and grow, licking the tree.

The tongues make my skin feel less hard. I feel it on my hands and face.

Now it is running along the ground eating all around me. Going toward our cave.

It is eating all around me. I run alongside it trying to capture the snake with my hands, but it turns them red and bites my skin. My feet cannot stop it. It eats the hair off my legs. Biting as it licks.

The white snake and blood tongues are now bigger than I am.

They continue to grow around me.

I see my people, coming out of the hill and start running. Arms in the air, hair streaming.

Running to the big water.

We have always run to the big water when the loud light from the sky has made the white snake and blood tongues appear.

There is nowhere to turn. The snake circles me.

Dancing and keeping me away from the big water.

I can see the girl running so fast to the big water.

The blood tongues will not let me go to her.

I grab sticks to fight the white snake.

I hear noise come out of my mouth.

I see the one-footed man hobbling to the water.

The girl runs past him.

The white snake chasing them both.

The tongues now eating my legs.

The snake now engulfs me.

There is nowhere to go. Nowhere to go.

"What? What?"

You'd think after all this time my fingers wouldn't get sore. Perhaps it's the springtime affecting them so. The impending rains and offsetting breeze from the river let the damp chill creep into my hands like a thief in the night. Similar to the one who keeps stealing our eggs. I'll catch that red-tailed rascal soon. Father taught me how to make a great trap for small vermin. Of course, he had to, being a man of the fields. Now that I think of it, must be the swinging door on the trap that isn't working right.

He never really thought he belonged in the fields, digging and scraping away with his large calloused body. Hands and shoulders rubbed raw from the yoke harness early in the spring. Labor as your parents did, doing what they taught you, working the land, the ledger, the fishing net.

His stoic face is burned into my memory the day when we were sitting at the table having late afternoon tea, taking a break from the harvest, when I told him what I actually wanted to do with my life. What I believed my destiny held for me. Now that I look back at it, I'm sure it sounded incredibly daft. Sitting with a man who had no doubt spent many of his first days bundled to Grandmum as she busied herself stripping vegetables, wringing chicken necks, darning socks for my 12 aunties and uncles on the family farm. She and Granddad determined to cut a life out of the earth.

After the initial shock wore off I think he understood, and quite frankly, agreed with me. I explained the many times he hadn't noticed the intricacies with which I had completed my ordained tasks. He wholeheartedly agreed my attention to detail was far beyond others in the community.

If you had been an observer during the conversation, you would have only had to look at the tea mugs to see the physical difference between us. His sleeves, still rolled up to the elbows, displayed well-muscled forearms and scarred hands from countless hours of chores and Sunday cricket. He manhandled the tea mug as steam rolled off the surface like the fog upon a stream in early springtime. Then the stranger would glace at the same physical features I possess and notice more of a delicate nature, designed for detailed work, versus the blunt requirements of a farm. No doubt I had inherited my mother's features, God rest her soul.

He accepted my decision, not lightly at first, but knew I had the gift of working leather. Over the course of the last several years his eyesight began to fail so I was placed in charge of mending all of the equipment, particularly the harnesses and horse tack, which had aged or snapped during use. My sisters could have done it, but my speed and accuracy won me the job and they were assigned other labors.

It's hard to remember when I first became infatuated with my current occupation. Perhaps, as a child, it was watching the nobles in all their finery. Being the dreamer that I am, I'd envision them gliding about a ballroom or a church gathering, presenting family members. Bows and curtsies abound, hands delicately presented and covered with the finest gloves one could offer. But yet, flesh never touching. The material of the glove having absorbed the pure magnetism and animal instinct the true hand-to-hand contact first provides. Strange how these things happen. I often wish I had written down my thoughts as a youngster, for the depth of some of them make me think I was truly off my rocker. Many of my ponderings never made it from my mind through my fingers onto a piece of parchment.

Even to this day, these abstract thoughts cross my mind as I sew new gloves for the well-to-do, or neighbors who have sweated through their only pair. The mounds of leather and wool within my shop are always welcome walls of solitude during my contemplative moments. My children often break the silence and my concentration with their bursts of energy and curiosity invading my mental fortress. Almost always a welcome invasion, almost.

As opposed to my earliest daydreams, the thoughts of my children's future accompany my hands as I cut, sew, and stitch. The years have not been easy on us after having lost two tender souls. Those premature departures ripped our hearts and souls apart flinging them into the dark ground beside each precious child.

Black Death is no stranger here, but that never makes it any less painful to watch God's fingers snuff out a candle so freshly lit. The Almighty has His plans, as I did, as most of us do. My aspirations to lead my community now almost a full-time obsession.

Oh, but the taxes have begun to weigh heavily upon my mind. Keeping the boys in school is so important to our station, but who will follow my occupation? Will my twin princesses make it through the first part of their young lives, unlike their sisters? Oh Lord, these are my deepest thoughts.

These dark thoughts are quickly erased by my children's playful natures. The musical laughter prior to the missus serving dinner is an absolute joy. It's a blessing watching my wife as her hands busily prepare a meal, eyes trained on the boys scampering about, trying not to run over their sisters. Always including the girls as obstacles during the chase. It's most certainly well-orchestrated chaos, as I supply the bellowing admonishments and occasional ear twists. Their energy lifts us all.

Mercy, what laughter they bring! I know at some point the ringleader of this devilish bard will sit down and tell me his true thoughts about seeking his fortune. Much like I did with my father. As much as I would cherish it, I doubt he will be the one to follow in my footsteps. Even at the age of seven he has a gift for storytelling and quick-witted retorts that leaves us in tears.

Just last night, he and his brother were the main actors in a pre-supper play about two country gentlemen who came across an ox, much like our own, stuck deep in the mud. Little Joan, the third player, was dressed as the beleaguered ox.

The gentlemen flounder in the muddy bog, pushing and pulling the ox but to no avail. A wondering maiden, player four "Miss Elizabeth", in her Sunday finery, stumbles upon this hilarious scene only to fall madly in love with the eldest of the two gentlemen. This maiden is none other than the teenaged good Queen Bess. The comedy ends happily ever after for the star-crossed lovers as announced by the leading actor himself, the quintessential, most desirable, talented, Sir Willie Shakespeare of Strafford upon Avon!

Mary and I were streaming tears of laughter shouting *Bravo! Bravo to the future King William!* while the young Shakespeare troop bowed and curtsied to their adoring crowd.

I see the dreamer in our Willie. What shall William become? What shall he become?

The Ring

One of my earliest memories is of seeing the rainbow form and dance across the room, then the ceiling, and back to the room again. Sparkling flashes of light coming from her finger. My mother's ring had a mesmerizing effect on me. As the light streamed through the windows on a bright morning it headed directly for her delicate beautiful hands, asking the ring to dance. And my goodness, it did!

Once Mom recognized my fascination with colors, she would always put on a show, both her voice and eyes laughing with true joy at my amazement. Her eyes, burnt caramel in color, not brown or black, but a light brown, had tiny, tiny flecks of green swimming on top of deep caramel pools. Even as a little kid, I can recall countless strangers commenting on her gorgeous eyes.

We met that son of a bitch on the city bus. I must have been six or seven at the time. Same old comment as he slouched across from us in his ratty short-sleeved tee shirt, tattoos complementing his ragged clothes. He leaned over getting as close as he could to my Mom's face, staring deep into her eyes, then leaned over in front of me, grabbed my chin pulling my face up so he could look at my eyes. I distinctly remember exactly what he said, "Too bad Lit'l Missy, if you had eyes like your Momma's, you'd rule this town."

My mother began standing as I pushed his greasy hand away, trying to forget the feel of his gritty fingers touching my skin. The stanky smell of weed and alcohol lingered as he pushed himself back across the bus aisle, belching a smoker's guttural chuckle.

I watched him watching Mom until the next stop when she grabbed my hand yanking my arm almost out of the socket, dragging me off the bus. It was confusing as this wasn't the food pantry stop we usually get off at. We waited ten minutes in complete silence and jumped back on the next bus just to go down ten blocks to the pantry stop. That was weird.

Two days later, this dude reappears, except this time he was prepared. Not as stoned, his A game ready to go. Not understanding my instincts were taking over, I watched my hands tremble as they tightly gripped my favorite book. Thinking the whole time, *"Don't talk to him, Mom, don't talk to this guy."* But she did, all the way to our stop, where he got off the bus with us.

If I had only really known what was going on, I

would have distracted the conversations some-how. I still blame myself for not stepping in. Maybe I was just too young.

He treated me all right for a while. Basically, like excess baggage you need for a short journey. He never laid a hand on me. No external bruises to speak of, no broken arms, no black eyes.

Mentally? Well, that's why we're talking, isn't it?

For the three years they were together, he picked off my real confidence like a military sniper. Eroding my self-esteem with razor-sharp com-ments for my ears alone. I never said anything to my momma because I wasn't certain what his com-ments meant or if he was being serious or not.

He sure as hell was serious, working some sort of plan. Perhaps I can describe how confusing his comments were with an example. This guy had tat-toos across the top of each hand. The right hand read "Jesus" and the left read "Lives". A two-headed serpent interwoven between the letters.

When I could finally read well, this sentence made no sense to me. I knew who Jesus was, the priest at the food pantry taught us about His kind-ness and love. So why would a guy who believes "Jesus Lives" always be jabbing a needle into his arms and hands? My mind's eye can still see that two-headed serpent dance as his hands squeezed my mother's arms, helping her get the big rubber band off her arm after the bubbling tar took hold.

As soon as the snake finished its dance, I knew I was on my own. I'd read my favorite books, play with my family of dolls, and when I could find the clicker, usually being clutched in his limp fingers, I'd turn on cartoons until one of them came back to reality.

My favorite pastime was gently slipping Momma's ring off her finger and wearing it around the house. If it was daytime, I'd find the sunniest spot and make the rainbows dance. I loved hiding in those colors, so bright in the middle, but fading so finely at the edges it wasn't offensive. Some things end so fast it makes me angry. But not my rainbows. They would end quietly, like a soft summer's rain that magically evaporates.

Here is where the problem began.

My mother lost her job again and we had to start going back to the pantry and using stamps. Well, this asshole, my favorite new word, now that I know what it means, took our book of stamps and sold them to buy drugs. They got in a huge fight, yelling back and forth, which ended in the traditional "Let's make up" groping session. Of course, he got his man purse out and lit up the spoon. The stuff took hold and they were both draped over the couch, like his well-used filthy shirt.

It was time to see my rainbows. I gently took Mom's hand, slipped her ring off, and found where the sun was smiling.

Oh, the summer show was beautiful! Blues dancing with reds, purple cutting in, jealous of the time the red had taken. The magic the ring created was magnificent!

Hearing my mother coming back to life, I slipped the ring off and headed toward the living room. I tripped on the corner of the old rug and the ring launched into the air, catching the sunshine as it tumbled. With two quick bounces, it fell into the floor grate in the corner of the hall. It was quickly swallowed up, making metal tinkling sounds and then going silent.

I had no idea what to do, so I did and said nothing.

"Is that how the fight started?" the officer asked.

"Yes, sir, it is. After they both came to their senses, my momma realized her ring was gone," I filled in.

Did I tell you it belonged to my grandmother? She brought it with her when she immigrated to America as a teenager. She and Poppie used it as her engagement ring. It's been in the family for a long, long time.

This was the first time I had ever seen my mother get physical with this guy. She kept pushing him in the chest around and around the living room. He swore he'd never steal anything to buy dope. Of course, Mom knew better, just look at our food stamps.

As for me, I was too scared to say anything about the ring, so I stayed hidden in the corner watching this frightening scene play out.

Mom pushed this guy over the couch, I think he was still stoned, and chased him around the kitchen throwing anything she could find at him, yelling louder than I had ever heard before.

Asshole tripped over the same old rug I had and crashed into the coffee table smashing his head right on the pointy corner. He hit the floor real quick.

He was about from me to you. The blood from his head was making a pool, like spilled milk on the table, and it began running toward me. His greasy head was facing the other way, but his skinny arm was reaching out to me. His fingertips clutching the wooden floor, the "Jesus" tattoo and serpent's head were doing the herkie-jerky dance and then stopped. He just laid there.

"My momma scooped me up and ran into the kitchen and then called 911."

"That's all I remember, Officer…"

The Walk

How many times over the years have I done this?

"The Father, the Son and the Holy Spirit, Amen" my hand trailing across my chest reaching for the railing. The harsh early winter air nipping as the breeze began to pick up. Knuckles stiffening, right knee beginning to protest.

Still can't believe the damn cow caught me off guard and kicked me and the brimming bucket of milk. What is it with her? We're the closest of friends. Constant early morning talks, complaining, yearning, confiding, while her milk streams forth making the tin bucket sing. Then she goes and kicks the stool, knocking me, the milk, and my pride into the dirt.

Well, she must feel the stress in my hands. Perhaps I was a bit rough now that I think of it. Another turn coming to an end, but not yet completed. It's never over till the last bit of cargo is unloaded and secured. Then it's over, another journey in the books. Thank God.

Whooo, a sharp gust raises a chill on my skin. My fingers gently stroke my hair back into place.

I'm enamored with how the beloved, cursed wind plays with my hair. When it has the mind, it can make me look like I've brushed it for hours, waiting patiently for the last strand to fall into place. Then it can be more playful, tossing and flipping it to and fro, leaving me looking like an ancient sea-witch from the depths of hell. Ironic.

Quietly studying the jagged scar on my right forefinger, my mind takes me back to my awful slip on the ice on this very spot. Hand darting to the railing steadying my feet. Not realizing the smallest metal shard was standing at attention just under the railing waiting to complete its mission of fileting my finger wide open. Droplets of blood decorating the black ice instantaneously. That nasty cut kept me from finishing the needlepoint commemorating his voyage.

No matter, I temporarily framed it anyway. His eyesight, as well as my own, is starting to fail, leaving the missing details lost in a sea of stitches. Most men don't appreciate the intricacies of a fine piece of homespun art. He did miss them, my finger healed, and I tacked in the date right before framing: 1839.

My goodness time goes quickly, married almost 23 years now. I fondled the locket around my neck and slowly pulled it from the collar of my dress, as I always do. My thumb gently maneuvering the latch to release the cover.

There you are, my dear. So handsome so many years ago, standing stoically for your tin-type. Remember? I had just cut your long flowing hair and unkempt beard. You had let both grow wild on your first 12-month turn, vowing not to cut a hair until you returned. And you didn't.

You may not believe it, but that is my favorite memory as a newlywed.

Me, standing behind you, daintily handling each of your flowing locks with my young fingers. Those hands having so little experience in life. No hardships, no children, no worry. So young. Slowly snipping cautiously not wanting our strangely intimate time to end.

I have reflected on that precious moment so often, realizing now it was the first time you ever shared your life's dreams with me. Your true dreams. How we would raise a family, become leaders in our community and stewards in the church.

I can still feel your hand upon mine even now. You gently grabbed my hand, your deeply calloused fingers upon my soft skin, and you told me how you dreamed of being a leader of men. One of the most honorable occupations known to humankind. Whether you knew it or not, you started to squeeze my hand tighter and tighter as you explained how all of the great men in the Bible had to earn the respect of those following them. Making the same commitment, disciplining them, and above all, sacrificing the same, if not more, than those souls in your care.

Then you slowly and quietly let go, reaching behind you to pat me so gently with your hand of steel. The same hand which would make those very dreams a reality.

The sacrifices? Yes, we've done this time and again over these long years. While you were out there changing the world, I was left here to pick up the pieces and carry on. Such sharp little cutting pieces.

Holding dearly to our two children as they passed on. So young, so innocent. How could I ever tell you the shadow covering my heart as they left this world?

Next was your father, asking for you, calling for you, envisioning you as he let go of his precious life. My Lord, he was proud of you. I can still hear it in his voice as he spent his last breath longing to see you.

My mother and father passing as well during your absence. Having toiled alongside many families living in our fishing town, they both understood my pain, my loneliness. My dreams of our future didn't include thoughts of such gut-wrenching emotional experiences. Surviving many God-forsaken winters. Longing to know where you might be. So many things you've missed, my love. So many things.

My hands gripped the rail. Squeezing and squeezing until my arthritic knuckles popped. One thought repeated, plaguing my mind.

Where are you?

Have the depths of your ocean finally claimed her prize?

Has the one whale, your nemesis, finally bested the man I love? Or has your crew finally mutinied during your obsession to hunt down the great white whale?

I gently hug myself, like you have many times, trying to bring both warmth and comfort to my aging body and mind. Tired, straining eyes searching the horizon for your ship.

Where are you, my captain, where are you?

Come home to me one last time.

My fingers trailed off my shoulders as I turned from my lonely post on the widow's walk of our home, his castle, my prison, to start another long lonely day of waiting.

The Mighty Oak

Like the Mighty Oak, he stood in front of all of us. His harsh and loving hands cupped and squeezing in rhythm with his intense hushed voice. His knuckles turning white as he stressed the point of our existence, his existence, my existence.

Candlelight illuminated his face as he towered above us. I'm sure he could only see dark black and brown bloodshot eyes staring back at him, drinking in all the hope he touted.

Hope in this miserable world? When the spirit would take him like this his arms and hands flailed around in cadence with his words and us farm folk wouldn't flinch at all. As a matter of fact, most would start to draw closer, like young children listening to their favorite bedtime story.

My Lord we were hungry for hope, love and a reason. Yes, a reason. A reason to continue on with this blessed miserable life.

When no one was around, I loved teasing the dog out by the big house. Chained to the mighty oak, running back and forth just barking and a barking as I threw stones at him. He didn't understand there was another world out there just waiting. The chain, the tree, and his small patch of dirt was all he knew. It was all I knew, right now. I'd heard stories of what lay beyond our small plantation my soul was chained to. The stories elders told of the land they grew up in, what it looked like, what it smelled like, the animals they'd hunt. It was all beyond these cotton fields.

How dark is man's inner being to enslave another? What sins did we commit to inherit such a heavy burden? Will the God mentioned in our tiny cabin really save us in the end? On many days my faith is shaken to the core. Preacher's face and belief appear in my mind's eye as his words from last night ring in my head.

I begin softly humming to the rhythm of my own footsteps which are leading me to today's back-breaking tasks...

Sinners don't let this harvest pass, hmmm hmm, hmmm hmmmm. Left foot draggin behind the fall of my right.

Oh Sinners, don't let this harvest pass, my calloused hands softly clap, *hmmm hmmmm.*

Sinners don't let this harvest pass, I hum out loud for the first time.

And die and lose your soul to cast, hmm humm.

Nope that makes no sense. My hands continue the rhythm with my walking beat. For they were hanging by my side, baskets strapped to my back, brothers and sisters carrying the tools.

And die and lose your soul at last, hmm, hmm.
Yes Sir, yes Sir.
Sinners don't let this harvest pass, hmm, hmm.
Sinners don't let this harvest pass, hmm hmm.
Sinners don't let this harvest pass!
And die and lose your soul at last, hmm hmm.

My oldest sister chided me for singing before we got to the field. My fingers absent-mindedly started clicking with each footstep. The words taking over my mind, seeing him preach in the shadows of the cabin. "Redemption!" he called to his captive sheep, I hear it ringing in my head so clearly, my hands now clasped together squeezing, pulsing like his. I can feel it, I can feel it, right here, right now. Redemption does live! My thumping heart picking up as my mind grasps the moment. The Lord's grace transcends our life!

I know that my redeemer lives, hmmm, hmmm.

I know that my redeemer lives, hmmmm hmmm.

Oh, I know that my redeemer lives.

So, children don't let this time to pass, hmm hmmm.

Sinner don't let this harvest pass, oh yea, oh yea, hmmm, hmmm.

The sharp barking bought me out of my trance. There he is, the dog chained to the tree. I bent over to sweep up a rock. My fingers touched it, bobbled it and dropped it. I clutch at it again and almost fall over from the weight of my load. Then they closed around a flat sharp rock, a bit bigger than a pebble. It fit perfectly between my thumb and forefinger, one I'd choose to skip across the river.

I slowly take aim and catch his eye. My Lord, he wasn't being vicious, he was calling me, communicating something urgent. Like the morning dawn's light, I saw it, we were one. Oh my Lord, we were the same kindred spirts, one and the same. Both chained to the tree of life. Choosing to see what we wanted.

Sinning dog on that old oak tree, hmmm, hmmmm.

I'm a sinning dog chained on life's cruel tree, hmmm hummmm.

Oh, Sinner see that cruel tree, hmmm hummm, oh yea.

Where Christ he died for that dog and me, hmmmmm ummmm.

My hand relaxed and the rock tumbled to the ground as my new-found kindred spirit stopped barking. How could I not see it before? Was it my imagination or did the sun just get brighter? Almost having to cover my eyes, realizing the blinding light was emanating from within, filling my entire being with true hope and gladness which had not existed only steps before.

The Mighty Oak tree we're chained to is the very one His cross was fashioned out of; it's flesh feeling the nails as did our Saviour's hands and feet.

So many on our farm had swung from the Oak.

Tragically hanging for wanting better in life. But now, right now, not so far from where I'm walking, men I don't know are deciding if our country would swing or be redeemed to a new life. So many men had unloosed their chains, having to bark for their beliefs. To have a say in the fate of others.

My hands met picking up the clap once again. My lips curling into a precious smile. This very moment in time was not lost on me. His gift from above not lost on me.

My God, he's a mighty man of war, hum-hmmmm. hummm hmmm.

Oh my God, he's a mighty man of war.

Watching my hands beating out a sharp clap, it was like they were someone else's. Was it the man I had witnessed last night clapping through me somehow?

My God, he's a mighty man of war. He is, he is.

Oh, us Sinners don't let this harvest pass.

Oh, Sinners don't let this harvest pass.

The time is ripe for us to hope, the Mighty Oak stands tall.

Yes, the Mighty Oak stands tall.

"Hey, little brother, what are you singing back there?"

Hmmm, hmmm, Oh Sinners, don't let that harvest pass. Hmmm, hmmmm.

Sinners, don't let that harvest pass.

The Baker's Son

Perhaps the pre-dawn chores with my parents gave me the love-hate relationship I have with the morning. I can vividly see my flour-covered hands plunging deep into the gigantic wooden bowl to begin the process. Momma or Papa would always spur me on, grabbing my worked dough, simultaneously giving me more to knead while they went on to create a baked masterpiece. The neighborhood standing in line for hours enjoying the thought of breaking our bread with their family. The same customers masquerading as our friends, rushing the door as the opening bell jingled, signifying the shop was open.

Wafting fresh smells, engulfing shallow souls. Yes, they'd pump Papa's hand, greeting him, the women lightly touching his arm. After ogling the morning's creations, the hemming and hawing commenced wholeheartedly. A cultural tradition, working the price. Coins would eventually cascade into my momma's outstretched palm. Such a hard-working, forgiving palm.

Beautiful gloves waved, hats doffed, and daily journeys continued. Yet, most of our customers chose not to recognize us outside the shop, which, was very confusing for a ten-year-old. Momma's standard retort, "God's will!". Papa's? "Fetch more wood for the stove."

All my younger siblings were oblivious to the way we were treated in town. Never crossed their minds at the butcher shop to wonder why our customers would stand next to us and say nothing. Seven siblings, all younger, two sets of twins mixed in the brood, all scampered about our shop daily avoiding chores somehow.

I understand now. I had thought I understood for years. My resentment festered for years. Carrying the load for my brothers and sisters always clouded true clarity and absolute understanding.

The Dream.

It was one of many recurring dreams of my youth. Making its appearance often, wanting, begging, for my understanding. It offered the key to a hidden door which my fingers were too afraid to hold. I'd just stare at the key, refusing its message. It was so, so simple. I was looking too hard. Just like Papa rifling through the shop searching for his glasses when the whole time they were perched on his covered head.

Strangely enough, The Dream always started with the sweet smell of pastry dough. Until I began researching about people like myself, I thought I was the only one whose dreams had smells. But it isn't uncommon. Dirt, filth, acrid smell of burning, and flowers, are some of the common smells in dreams. And, of course, hearing in dreams isn't unusual. The mind is so adept at capturing the essence of an original sound, that when dreaming, it's like you are hearing the noise for the very first time. After so many years I still dream in German. Amazing! However, I digress.

The Dream. I'm standing in the shop massaging light pastry dough for Momma, being delicate, knowing she is making fancy cakes or pastries for our society's upper crust. My shirt sleeves kept falling down over my forearms, like they're trying to hide something or they're too shy to be seen. As much as I try, I can't pull them up like Papa does, keeping them out of the flour and dough.

As I lift my hands out of the bowl, my nails begin turning as black as coal. The ominous stain spreads from my fingertips to my fingers, then hands and all the way up my arms. Watching myself in the dream, I lift my arms in front of me. Looking past them, I see my reflection in the shop window, a tattered boy covered in filth and flour. Hair askew, teeth missing, holes in my apron. I plunge my hands back into the dough and the dark color drains from my body replaced by the floury white dust making all things normal again. Momma's voice, clear as a bell, and never changing, would chide "Keep your hands in the bowl, keep your hands in the bowl, it's the only thing keeping you alive."

A high-pitched male voice would cackle from in front of the counter singing "*He's a little dough-boy. Baking for his life. Bake, doughboy, bake, bake, doughboy, bake!*" This voice, never accompanied by a face, would trail off in a shrill laugh causing me to bolt upright in my bed, hand fumbling for the light to break the darkness.

Strangely enough, of all my fright-filled dreams, I didn't want this one to go away. Hearing my Momma's and Papa's voices, as clear as village church bells, is something I wanted to hold onto. Particularly as Father Time started to pick at their images. I actually treasure the first part of my dream as it ushers in sweet smells and family voices.

I've only shared this dream with my youngest sister. While discussing it I have the strange physical effect of my knuckles and wrists aching from kneading the dough, particularly as I'm told to plunge my hands into the bowl time and again. My sister only asks me about The Dream when we share coffee and pastry in my shop after synagogue, where we both feel comfortable, safe, at home. She would have been approximately four at the time of my dream as she was the younger of the second set of identical twins. Her experiences and dreams are drastically different than mine. Most she'll never share. The emotional scars I will never truly fathom but the physical reminders running over the course of her body, particularly her palms, speak volumes about her nightmares.

The memories of our family have faded from her mind, but the smells of my bakery take her back to those special times of scampering through Papa's shop playing tag or chasing the family cat.

Our dreaming conversation always ends with "But what does it mean, this dream of yours?"

Well, now we know.

I hope and pray thousands of lost souls will thank me for finally accepting the extended key in my dreams. Not burying the memories deep in my being, extinguishing my parent's voices or disregarding the smells of so many years ago. So much lost. Most importantly, for not erasing the sing-song voice taunting me for the last 64 years. My eyes have begun to betray me but my ears have not. God's will, they have not.

"Sir, please continue," my lawyer said.

I steadied my now ancient hands on the worn wooden railing.

"On the sixth of November, two months ago, I was watching my grandson for the day. It was a special occasion as he is now old enough to learn to make our family's famous chocolate Bobka. My clerk had to take a quick break, so Joseph and I were tending to our morning customers. My goodness, he was covered with flour from head to toe. Such a young rascal, that one."

My arm, now taking on a life of its own,

seemed like it weighed 60 pounds alone as it lifted my shaking hand. My fingers, not covered with flour or dirt, pointed across the courtroom.

"That man came into my bakery and ordered a loaf of bread. My grandson placed his loaf in the paper bag. He paid Joseph and began softly singing in a very high-pitched sing-song voice, "*He's a little doughboy, baking for his life. Bake, doughboy, bake, bake, doughboy, bake…*"

"Four long years I baked for this man and his kind." My voice trailed off as my mind found the mental key and unlocked the door. Arthritic hands adjusted my locks as years flooded forth and began to tumble in place. How could I forget this voice which ended my childhood along with many others?

I pulled up my shirt sleeve slightly and caressed the tattoo of my faded blue numbers serving as a testament to God's will.

The Herd

There it is.

Only took six weeks to finally poke through. My fingertip stared back at me as though it didn't know what I was talking about. Just in time for winter, too. I'd worn these gloves for over a year now. Not too many stains from running the presses back in Virginia. They were fairly new at that point.

My fingernail was a horrible sight. Chipped and ground down to the tip, crusty dirt underneath. At least Mother's not here to chastise my ungentlemanly appearance.

I'll need to patch this glove today and begin to think of the kind of hide I'll use to cover my hands as the winter rolls in. Something more durable, and most definitely thicker than the fine leather I'm using right now.

Winter's not long in coming. I can feel the stiffness in my knuckles where that damn colt kicked me the first time I was shoeing him. If I'd known what trouble he'd cause in years to come I would've put him down right then and there. As I trace the old scar on the back of my arm with my exposed fingertip, I can still feel the vice-like grip of his teeth tearing out a substantial piece of flesh. Damn, it was an excruciating bite, but oh, he was as a quick as a rattler, I didn't even see it coming.

The biggest wound he gave our family was throwing Father into the rock wall. He crumpled like a rag doll as he became one with the muddy earth. I watched him clutch at the rocks with his big English hands, the beefy hands of a yeomen, but no strength came. I immediately knew something was terribly wrong. Gasping, gurgling, and floundering in the mud, while the damn colt skipped off shaking the saddle loose. In those few seconds he broke both my father's and family's backs.

Brother wasn't ready to take over the family printing business. He was just learning how to set the plates properly when father passed. Benjamin resembled mother's side of the family; small-boned, dainty hands, and very quick with a sharp retort. His lack of brute strength and other interests slowly began the end of the family business. He was ripe for politics, making trouble for the crown with his cartoons and underground writing. He'll do well in his efforts as the colonies grow.

My hand gently stroked my gelding's steaming neck, "Could that have been nine years ago?"

Gus's efforts warmed my palms as I laid them under his mane. I leaned slightly and pushed my hands forward urging my steed up the last part of the rolling mountain. The terrain along the Missouri was vastly different than the squalor fast becoming the new town of St. Louis. My Lord those trappers are a rough crowd. Amazing how I can't remember seeing one without a bottle, knife, gun, or a woman of ill-repute in their blood-stained hands. Not a pleasant crowd if your nose is easily offended. Some of their experiences of trading with the native Indian folk comes in handy in this part of the country.

Riding through the last piece of dense woods I shielded my eyes from the newly setting sun.

"My God, there they are!" I actually gasped out loud. Groping for my spyglass, I had to see these creatures as closely as I could for I had only heard tales to this point. I extended the dented, marred tube and placed it against my eye.

My gelding caught their scent as I tried to count the roaming majestic creatures. The musky odor bothered him as both his curiosity and fear began to take hold. I soon lost track of counting as the massive herd meandered across the plain.

Look at the coats on those beasts, no wonder the trappers were enthralled with them. Legend has it the local tribes have followed this very herd for as long as anyone can remember. Tying their very existence to this creature for food, clothing and shelter. How in the world could they bring these beasts to the ground with a lance or arrow? Those bulls must weigh 1,200 pounds and I can't imagine a hunter could get very close. The horsemanship of the native plainsmen was nothing less than exquisite, legendary even. Fearless, balanced, speed beyond compare. I yearn to see them on the hunt.

Just then I noticed my hands were actually trembling, not from the cold night setting in, but from the sheer thought I was witnessing something few patriots had ever seen before. How could I explain, truly describe in word or story, the majesty of thousands upon thousands of animals roaming, existing, creating life together?

I stowed my spyglass and slid out of the saddle to quickly check my rigging. My hands hefted the girth, gaining one more notch. Gus's heart was pounding as quickly as my own as we started, feeling the unquenchable need to become one with the herd. Get as close as possible to these animals, to touch the matted thick brown coat. The hides the French and Indians wore in St. Louis were magnificent.

I hadn't felt this thrill of adventure since sneaking under the Tavern table and listening to the arguments the local farmers, calling themselves Revolutionaries, were having about how the Crown was outreaching its authority in the 12 colonies. Benjamin was so involved in that political nonsense. Better him than me.

If only he could see this sight, thousands of beasts wading in and out of the muddy banks of the Missouri: cows pushing calves along to fresher grass, young bulls jostling one another to gain position in the herd for the next breeding season. The older bulls, like sentries, posted toward the outskirts of their family, leading the way for this mass of existence they had created.

I loosed the powder horn from my saddle, covered the opening with my exposed fingertip to ensure the powder had remained dry after our last river crossing and quickly loaded my trusted musket.

I patted Gus on the neck to signal our departure onto the next phase of our adventure. I felt his muscles quiver beneath me as he, too, knew our pursuit would be one of a lifetime.

In my mind I had already begun to write the letter home to Benjamin about my first encounter with the northern continent's wild buffalo.

The Statesman

Damn this blotting. Now it's all over my cuff and hands. I never seem to keep ink off of my fingers. Always leaks deep into the cracks of my stained fingers. When did my fingers get this bony? I gently caressed my temples and adjusted my reading glasses, beckoning to my loving, ever-present wife. Such a tempest in our home as of late.

"Please bring me another handkerchief to blot my hands. I seem to have made a mess."

Then it happened, the black ink on my hands ushered in the image of that black man's hand in mine. His was rough and wood-like from years of inhumane work on the docks in Baltimore, missing a finger from a loading accident. What immense physical pain must have accompanied that life-changing event. How different are they really, the physical and mental pains? One over quickly only to leave the other to languish for days, years, even a lifetime.

It's interesting how a disfigured hand feels in your own when you shake it. It's enveloped, yet for the most part still strong, not wanting to give up its identity. My mind quickly moved past the impairment to the human being extending it, knowing we are joined in an unforgettable moment in time. But yet, wasn't it just a finger? A physical appendage the loss of which can be dealt with? However small, a tragic individual loss, nonetheless.

Catastrophic losses do seem to plague me. Too many times I've dreamed puzzling events only to have them blossom in some form or fashion. The echo of foreshadowing steps following behind me each day. Particularly after Gettysburg just six weeks ago. Casualties, up to 18,323 and counting. What in the world will I say to consecrate such hallowed ground? My mind cannot fathom the physical and mental carnage of only a few short days. Destiny having selected such rich farmland for perhaps one of the fiercest battles between brothers to date. Can our country survive? When will we realize the grave injury we are inflicting upon ourselves? Not being able to slow this mad runaway train.

My God. The Lord and Savior hit me with a thunderbolt as my thoughts tightened around the slim quill now poised in my bear-sized hand, nib twitching just above the unstained parchment. Thoughts grappling in my brain for alignment, pushing and shoving for the first to become a legible sentence. The mangled hand of a poor black man and one of the most horrendous battles in history strangely running parallel as harbingers of a unique future.

That's it! For it wasn't just his index finger bluntly taken from him, but his soul. His very being was changed. His deep set, mahogany eyes told me as much. As he clutched my shoulder and pumped my hand during a brief moment, a glimmer, just a faint light, shot through his eyes, colliding with the inner pain torturing me.

There, standing before me, in its most raw and unabashed nakedness, was Hope. This human being, regardless of how badly treated by our Union, had Hope in our future, his future, his children's future. He saw me as the guardian of this most cherished newly flickering light. So fragile an infant's whispering voice could easily extinguish it.

This concept was so daunting it felt as if two farmer's hands were throttling the air from my chest and windpipe. At that very moment I became truly engaged in our Civil War, my civil war.

Like a forgotten match searing the fingertips for a microsecond, this revelation broke the logjam of words in my mind, allowing such pure clarity of thought to gush forward through my quill, I could hardly keep pace with the torrent.

All men must be *free, truly free, truly emancipated* to live the best life they could muster.

The first words magically appeared at the end of my blackened fingertips, my lips curling briefly, wondering what Seward and Welles would think. This will ease our divided house.

I must capture the fleeting essence of my mind, the crystal-clear reality lying there in front of me, waiting to be picked up.

"July 1862 Preliminary Proclamation, President Abraham Lincoln."

> *All persons held as slaves within any State or designated part of a State, the people whereof shall then be in rebellion against the United States, shall be then, thenceforward, and forever free.*

I laid my pen gently into its holder and flicked open my pocketknife, realizing my nib had gone flat again. This phrase having been captured, I released my mind to begin scratching the surface of how I was going to enforce such a God-given right. So simple, how can it not be acknowledged by all? Yet here in my own house beliefs were divided.

My own family was the epitome of this struggle. Mary's family believing and needing slave labor for a viable business to flourish. Richard, now sporting his splendid blue uniform, itching to join the fray that has claimed so many young boys and men. Oh, and my blessed Willie. His ghost accompanying me each day, the echoing sounds of imagined battles, him being the great general orchestrating heroic victories in the name of the Union.

His tiny knuckles worn raw as the final shots were fired. A historic moment, this house divided...

Absently scratching my beard, I felt the tempest in my mind began brewing, thoughts gathering like midwestern storm clouds seen miles away. The dark bold clouds signified my understanding of the action which must be taken. I must cripple the Confederacy by emancipating and protecting our Negro brethren both politically and militarily. Our countrymen, regardless of the soil on which they trod, must be free.

Yes, that was it, my quill once again took on a life of its own, fingers welcoming fresh ink with the fervent hope of changing the course of our great Nation.

The Hideaway

My finger caught the corner of the cupboard door, pulling it halfway open and then letting it clap shut; stinging the cut I had inflicted upon myself that morning. Why are those little pricks you get from a needle so painful? I hope the door shutting didn't wake Mother. She hates it when I sneak food in the middle of the night.

What else is there to do other than lie there wide awake thinking of him? Watching the shadows deepen while they creep across my ceiling in step with the night watchmen's rounds.

Mother says I have to realize he may be gone forever. As quickly as I brush the independent strand of hair from my eyes, I dismiss the thought, refusing to believe she may be right.

We shared our fleeting time together after church adjourned and the mounting heat of the day became demanding. I loved the feel of his hands when he stroked my hair. They weren't quite the hands of a man when we first met but were getting there. Permanently stained brown, a bit like those of his father, the town clockmaker, just a slight presence in the little tiny cracks around the sides of the knuckles. For most who weren't looking, I doubt they'd be seen at all. He'd hold my hair on display in front of both of us and we'd laugh and laugh about how the two chestnut colors matched so perfectly. I loved tracing those stained tracks in his fine callouses. Peeking, hiding, but ever-present.

While Father greeted his parishioners and Mother was busy getting food ready for the obligatory post-service lunch, we'd sneak off under the seven-year-old white oak for a sliver of privacy. I remember when my family planted the oak, celebrating my tenth birthday and the anniversary of Grand- father's passing. The oak's shade held many conversations of our future, his future, our envisioned family's future. My Lord, have things gotten complicated.

My handsome oak has grown. Strong, majestic, so proud of the many victorious battles against harsh Rhode Island winters. Much like our love, I know it's going to make it.

After I placed my dinner on the table, I laced my fingers together in prayer asking a kind and forgiving God for my love's return. This nightly routine has become quite a comfort, sometimes my only comfort, as the stillness of night crowds in around me. The dreadful thoughts of his journey make their way into my mind like the tide switching from high to low. Ever so subtly my thoughts change as my mental high tide makes itself known. Honestly, I don't think we understand these times we live in. So hard, so demanding of the soul. How did we get here?

As I slide my finger along the butter knife to capture the last of the crumbs, I heard a very small, very muffled sounds coming from the depths of the house; like the sounds you hear in many of these old New England houses. Perhaps a long-lost whaler's spirit coming home from Davey Jones' locker, seeking his long-lost family. I absently ran my palm across my forearm and felt the fine goosebumps rising to meet the racing heartbeat in my fingertips.

Like a moth to the flame, I followed the noise as it happened again. My thumb and forefinger gently meet in the ring of the pewter candle holder as it played host to a small stub still burning from my nightly quest to the kitchen. I hesitantly began creeping across the floorboards toward the cellar door and listened to the ancient planks groan in protest to my adventure. The creaks sounded like gunshots. No doubt like the ones my love is hearing on a daily basis on the battlefield.

I arrived at the door and hesitantly reached out to grasp the metal knob, its cold temperature calling my goosebumps to attention. It smoothly turned, making its small clicking noise.

The muffled noise stopped.

I held my breath and didn't move for what seemed like an eternity.

There it is again.

I pulled the door back ever so gently and stood frozen on the first of ten steps leading into the dank cellar. Do I have the courage to do this? Go into a greater darkness than the one in my troubled heart?

My hand reached out and felt the cool, moist wall. There are times in February when the bottom part of the wall actually gets covered with a fine frost. Not yet, though. As my light cascaded down the stairs the noise immediately hushed again.

What is that?

My arm swept in front of me and confirmed nothing was out of place. I could see my fingertips; they traced the wall as the last step greeted my chilled foot.

My heart leapt out of my chest as Father's treasured Bunker Hill war blanket fell from the back wall and crumpled to the floor.

I took one step closer and the illumination from my candle suddenly meet the eyes of another human being. I fell backward onto the step, my right fingers stung from the hot candle wax while my left arm caught the banister to support me.

Four eyes, peered out from under the stack of clothing in the corner. Ever so slowly a lily-white palm rose in the air to greet my horrified stare. It turned into a small sign as a women's forefinger touched her lips and pointed skyward and gently breathed *shhhhhh.*

In what has to be God's most cognitive realization of the speed in which time can move, I understood what was unfolding in front of me. To confirm my belief, a girl, so small and delicate in the light, left her mother's side and came to me with both hands outstretched, like old friends greeting each other after Sunday service.

I perched the candle on the shelf and knelt as this small soul placed her tiny hands in mine. Sweating, yet cool, and calloused. Well beyond a child of her age. Our eyes meet in the darkness of the cellar, our hideaway.

I looked down at our hands now intertwined, joined in a common journey, and even in that light I could make out the chestnut brown color running through the creases in her hands, matching the color of my hair.

At that very moment, I realized my love would be coming home to me.

Pen Pals

I love writing. Watching the smooth stroke of my pen flowing across the page in rhythm with each thought gives me the immortal feeling of capturing something no one can see until I will it so. Very powerful and bold to take that risk; letting people know what you think or perhaps giving them the idea they know what you think and feel.

There are times when I'm so deep into writing to you I don't realize how sore my left fingertip is and my hand is actually cramping with each word I write.

But, my precious friend, you already know that, don't you? Having been my most valued confidant for these 23 years. Through my most joyous times, and most painful, hateful really.

As I write today you totally understand. Pen Pals for life is what we agreed on after our first chance meeting in seventh grade. Even though I've moved around a lot with my Dad being a contractor for the military, we've kept up the daily tradition. My two greatest passions, memories if you will, till this point, are writing to you and sitting with Dad to build my first aircraft model. Who would have thought I would eventually design them?

Dad's technical knowledge regarding aircraft has always been a marvel. All day long he installs and troubleshoots sophisticated electronics for the Air Force's heavy bombers. He says it's like surgery sometimes, super-fine hand movements when you're soldering broken components, fuse banks and motherboards.

I've always tried to mimic his actions during the hours upon hours of building aircraft replicas. As you know, my favorite part is always painting the nose art on the WWII bombers. At first it was difficult because of the detail I had to muster. Creating those beautiful, well-endowed women, long, sensuous legs crossed, hair perfectly groomed, flying into battle with the men they love. Then it just happened, like the first trip on your bike without training wheels, their curves and lines just appeared.

I don't think I ever actually told you this before, and thank God you've never judged me, but painting the Memphis Bell replica is when I first realized it, detailing her bright red pumps, the ones popular in the mid 40s with the ribbons as laces. A small speck of "Ruby Red" paint (my favorite color) dripped onto my right fingernail. Something stirred in me. No, not the lustful feelings of a 13-year-old adolescent boy, but, if you can imagine, something deeper. A feeling I know you may not understand but then again perhaps you might.

It was as if I had awoken. At that moment I gently placed my paintbrush in its holder and lifted my hand, inspecting the small droplet pooling so perfectly on my fingernail. It sat there, defiant of gravity. Not dripping, not running. Perfect in its solitude, trying to tell me something.

It was almost funny because my knuckles were a bit banged up from seventh grade football practice. That speck of paint, marking its territory down by my cuticle, didn't care what the rest of my fingers looked like in comparison, or myself in its entirety. It only knew it was on a mission, sent from the inner depths of my bottle of "Ruby Red".

I choose to believe it was God's tiny spot of paint trying to guide me. And as you know, it took me years of running, exploring and hiding to figure it out. Painful heart-wrenching experiences I've written about many times. Perhaps tenfold in high school which was just confusing as hell for all of us. Four years of torment, utter torment. Mom always knew that period of life was difficult, because at some level, I know deep in my heart, she had some trouble during her teenage years as well. No doubt she is my parental soulmate. Dad is more like a maestro perfecting his gifted student.

College, as I've told you, was a true experience, in every sense of the word. Finding fulfilment in choosing an occupational path similar to my father's where I could put my fine dexterous motor skills to work. Not for the real-time war-birds in Iraq Dad worked on daily, but for something more creative. Where my burning desire could grow and flourish: Sculpting.

Sculpting for the art and sake of sculpting. Hands creating something from deep within. Letting ideas and feelings loose in the moment to run their course, taking on a form of their own. Never really knowing where they're going at the start. A vague idea, yes, but not a final, perfect idea. Clay submitting to the strength of my hands, feelings pulsing and driving to reach the final form. An idea set free.

True art. Aren't we all a form of God's hands creating true art? Do we have the remotest idea of the final outcome?

I wrote you my favorite expression of this emotional analogy a few years back. Perhaps the most accurate words about these feelings surfacing to the top of my soul.

"It was like a butterfly, new to the world, had just landed softly in my palm. I had the choice to let it fly away to create, multiply, and bless this world with its God-given beauty. Or I could choose to slowly pinch my fingertips upon its wings keeping it for my own pleasure. Just for me to look at and not share. I could push the tiny pins through its beautiful wings into the cardboard pallet which I had selected. Trapping its glorious beauty in a glass frame, looking out to see the world passing by. Never participating but always there for my personal pleasure."

I know I've written this passage to you time and again, and I thank you for not chastising me for the repetition. I know it takes precious time away from your day to read my thoughts. I truly thank you.

Today is the day I am choosing to let my beautiful creature fly. I'm telling you first, my friend, my pen pal, my journal. You deserve to know my decision because you have been with me from my awakening.

Today, I'm telling my parents what God truly created in me: A woman.

I am choosing to shed my masculine shell and pursue what my God was saying through one small defiant dot of "Ruby Red" paint which stood so lonely on my fingernail ten years ago.

It's time I let the sculpting of my essence continue in the fashion I now recognize.

I am beginning my transition.

Kneading Hands

Why does it always seem my hands are ice cold this time of day, especially when I meet a new family?

"I'm sorry my hands are so cold."

I feel the tingling heat as I vigorously rub my palms together, making a show of it, so the shocking feeling won't last too long.

"Glad to see you could both make it. Facing this challenge as a couple always lends to a great deal of positive energy on a long road."

Did that sound right? What's a long road? Are they going to read into that as if there is a shorter road, a very dark and unlit road?

Or will they choose to be the eternal optimists and believe their road will really end in a positive uplifting recital of "Hallelujah"?

Damn, for someone so intelligent I say some pretty stupid stuff.

Focus on the protocol, stay positive. You know more than they do, perhaps too much.

My God this couple is young. My hand absently caresses the locket Mom gave me. The etching on such a fine piece of gold sends tingles through my fingers, directly to my heart.

What was Dad thinking when he gave her the locket before departing to quell the Nazi hordes in Europe? Coming back years later with a left-hand bearing scars from pulling his friend out of a burning piece of twisted metal. Charred, melted flesh to forever remind him he was actually the lucky one.

Those wrinkled lines fascinated me. I always thought they looked like the mountainous terrain features on 3D maps I'd see in museums. All the peaks and valleys as they ran across the top of his hand and knuckles. Did God have some secret message burned into my dad's fingers? Maybe it was a map of nirvana or heaven or some secret place that had a life-easing treasure? Childhood thoughts...

Young lovers separated for four years. I can't stand to be away from my family at all. Four years! What love can endure. Amazing.

This young couple will experience separation. But only one of them will truly feel it.

I can still see my mother's eyes well up as she lay there, head so light it barely creased the pillow. Our hands intertwined like the long vines growing up an old tree. Her palms so soft and warm awaiting the Lord's Angel. Red Death having done it's work on her physical body. That devil couldn't touch her spirit. It was a shame the treatment left her with a slight tremor. It went away immediately when she'd pass along her daily blessing to the family.

How many times have I searched for the first physical signs of a life-changing mass? The tiniest of bumps masquerading as something innocent under soft skin.

My God, I hate my job. My God, I love my job.

I placed my back to her husband blocking his view and began my examination. I always think it's an uncomfortable time for a young partner to watch the love of his or her life go through the initial process. No doubt this couple's active. Both are lean, fit, athletic-looking. The enemy I'm searching for doesn't care about how active you are, lazy, rich or poor. It's extremely unbiased leaving a harsh trail of "Why me?" in its wake.

"Do you exercise daily?"

"That's excellent. I need you to keep up your Taekwondo as you go through this experience. There may come a time when you can't, particularly if there is reason for treatment, but until then it's critical."

Yea, I should have guessed martial arts. Hands well-muscled with a few very slight scars running across her knuckles where she's broken boards. Her ring finger looked as though she'd broken it at one point in time.

Time to start kneading. Be soft. Start at the top and work your way down. I find it interesting my new patients always flinch the first time I start their exam. They know my touch is coming, I know it's coming, I tell them it's coming. I suppose it's the realization the living nightmare is beginning. It's actually happening to them. Becoming a statistic is a terrifying fear.

Ok, upper portion is clear. Now move down toward the areola and nipple. Damn, there's the bump, trace it. Now over the top. Now underneath. Push, prod, see if you can move it at all.

Lost it. Circle back.

"Relax, we're almost done." God, this is terrifying for both of us.

There it is again. Alright. I think I can handle this one. Still the size of a small pebble.

I pray this one isn't a fast mover having tentacles like a vengeful McCracken, pulling her life down to the depths of the emotional ocean, where light doesn't exist.

Follow your left hand, transition to the right breast.

Keep your face warm, positive, stoic. Continue the deadly search.

"Breath. Please keep breathing for me. Relax if you can."

My God, I hope this breast is clean. The odds predict it will be for a first-timer. I pray they are right, I pray they are right.

Follow the path, start at the top, and work your way down.

Stop, retrace, and circle back. Breathe, nothing there, yet. Thank God.

Why is it I always envision my Grammy making bread when I'm doing this? Her hands were so gentle, particularly as we read my favorite books or when we moved pieces gracefully around the backgammon board.

But when she had dough in her hands? Man, she was unmerciful. Brutal, even. Kneading it to hell and back. But *ohhh*, that all faded away when she spread butter on a thick piece of warm toast.

Right side is all clear, my delicate fingertips report, like good soldiers returning back from a reconnaissance mission. Well done, troops, keep up the hard work.

"Ok, now for the news. There is a small mass in your left breast. By the size of it, my estimation is less than two millimeters. However, I need you to understand me, that is only an estimation and the mammogram this afternoon will let us know what the true size is."

"The positive news: Your right breast is clear. There are no signs of any issues whatsoever. I know both you and your husband have deep concerns and many questions, but if you can excuse me for two minutes, I'll be right back."

I lightly patted her shaking shoulder as I left the room and went directly to the bathroom across the hall.

Shutting the door quickly, I twisted the silver knob until I felt the click of the lock.

Leaning on the porcelain sink I found my looking glass. "Oh Sleeping Beauty, there you are."

Looking deeply into my eyes, my mother's eyes, I could see her reflection standing behind me. Gently rubbing my neck, telling me all would work out as "God planned it."

Like you, Mom? I sat by your side for three years, a professional in the oncology industry, and could do absolutely nothing as your body was racked with pain. Witnessing your progression into nothing but a skeleton.

But I'm way ahead of you, Mom. Ahh yes, the Big Fella put me on the fast track. My quaking hands came up to my face, then slowly back down to my own chest.

How could you, Lord? How could you plant two life-stealing lumps in my own chest? My heart bleeds for the women you choose to carry this illness. The messengers of our own mortality.

Why me? Why now? Two high school children, a husband out of work, a career on the rise?

Why me, you son of a bitch? I can't even bear to tell my colleagues of your choice. My selection to your varsity team.

Should I go outside my own practice for help?

Should I not tell anyone at all and just ride this runaway wagon toward the cliff?

Will I choose "Red Diablo" as my cocktail? I can hardly stomach the look and smell.

I must be at least Stage III.

I've got to make a choice soon. Have to.

Pushing on the porcelain sink, I can see my knuckles turning white as I leaned into the mirror.

Oh, I am so sick of this discussion already. I've got to tell someone soon or I'm going to explode.

I know, Mom, you fought it. I know I can as well. We can do this.

Now it's time to get back into the battle and let these young kids know what their options are.

I gently dabbed the tears from under my slightly puffy eyes.

My God, I look tired. Just wait.

Feeling the silver knob in my fingertips, the welcoming click signaled my parole from this tormenting situation, conversation, and predicament.

I headed back across the hallway.

"We can do this."

About the Author

Mark M. Dean and his family live in Southeast Ohio on a small horse farm nestled in the foothills of the Appalachian Mountains. His endeavors as an author, lyricist, and poet are fueled by childhood memories of many family tales and exploits regarding colorful characters in his clan.

Mark has had the pleasure of living in ten states, stretching from Rhode Island to Arizona, while also having lived and traveled abroad. His 20 years of military service involved 12 family moves which gave him keen insight into the importance of bonding through stories, songs and poems.

Mark struggled with childhood dyslexia and desires to pay back all those who helped him develop his imagination through reading and storytelling.

He has an undergraduate degree from Miami University and a master's degree from Ohio University.